SEX AND THE SINGLE SISTER

SEX AND THE SINGLE SISTER

FIVE NOVELLAS

MARYANN REID

ST. MARTIN'S GRIFFIN
NEW YORK

www.stmartins.com

Library of Congress Cataloging-in-Publication Data

Reid, Maryann.
    Sex and the single sister : five novellas / Maryann Reid.
       p. cm.
    ISBN 0-312-27498-X (hc)
    ISBN 0-312-30072-7 (pbk)
    1. Erotic stories, American. 2. African American women—Fiction.
3. Single women—Fiction. I. Title.

PS3618.E54 S4 2001
813'.6—dc21   2001019168

First St. Martin's Griffin Edition: June 2002

10 9 8 7 6 5 4 3 2 1

THIS BOOK IS DEDICATED TO
THE MEMORY OF MAMI GLORIA,
MY GUARDIAN ANGEL,
MY SECOND MOTHER

WE MISS YOU

I want to give lots of love and thanks to my mother, Veronica Reid, for having patience every time I changed my job or came to you with another crazy idea, for listening to my goals, and for raising me and my sister, Arlene, on your own.

I want to give thanks to my agent, Richard Curtis, for returning all my calls and E-mails "in a New York minute." And thanks to my editors: Glenda Howard—for showing so much enthusiasm in taking on this book!—and thanks to my new editor, Monique Patterson, for your commitment to its success.

I want to thank all the men in my life who have inspired me to write this book. Thanks to Wil for giving me the "real" male perspective and for always being honest when you knew I wasn't right. We've been through it all! Thanks to Jimmy "Mac" for staying up late nights trying to figure out why a good man like you was single for so long. Thanks to my ex, Shawn, for your help and for listening to me read my stories over late-night phone conversations. Who would've thought, huh? Thanks to those men I've dated for giving me something to laugh about as I look back.

Thanks to my girlfriends, who know who they are, for sharing their joys, worries, and pain about relationships.

Thanks to Lucy and Matilda for being like older sisters to me.

I want to thank my grandmother, "Mama," for reminding me what it means to be calm in life's matters.

Thanks to God for another blessing.

INTRODUCTION

○○
○○

Okay, girls, where will it be tonight? The club, the lounge, the networking event, the bar, or the comedy show? Whatever the place, there will be brothers there. Fine, tall brothers, suited down, preferably Armani or FUBU—whatever your taste is. Here it goes: He stares. You stare. He buys you a drink. You drink. You give your number. He calls. You go on a date. Now what?

I want to give you an intimate peek into the lives of five very successful girls in their twenties. Women of all age groups can experience the troubles these girls go through in trying to find the right man. Like most girls in their twenties, they are experiencing many things for the first time. Either out of a bad relationship, still in a new one, looking for a husband, or exploring their sexuality, it is in these experiences where they find themselves and evolve as women.

Farah, Alaya, Kenya, Alexis, and Waceera just don't want *any* man. They are black princesses and want their prince. They do not come from families with "old" money and their parents are not socialites. They just have big dreams, are high-achievers, and have paved their own way. Martha's Vineyard, international trips, tropical islands, and the Hamptons are their vacations of choice. They are not chickenheads, and the men they choose are definitely not scrubs.

These girls, though they live in different cities, travel in the same social circles and have great careers but empty personal lives.

Their stories are inspirational, funny tell-alls about the dating scene and making all the wrong moves. There are two sides to every story, and each girl finds her lesson. If you think you are the only woman who hasn't had sex since Clinton was in the White House, is suffering from "can't find a man" blues, has had a string of bad dates, dated somebody's daddy, or slept with your date's girlfriend, then read on. There is something to be learned in each story. Sometimes the truth hurts, and sometimes, well, it feels so damn good!

THE GIRLS

⸬

⸬ STORY ONE: FARAH

AGE: 24

CITY: Brooklyn, NY

DATING STATUS: "Caught up with somebody else's catch"

Farah, a junior correspondent for a local TV network, is a good girl at heart. She's a workaholic with no man. Her "situation" with a committed guy leaves her with a new outlook.

⸬ STORY TWO: ALAYA

AGE: 26

CITY: San Francisco, CA

DATING STATUS: "Carefully treading the dating waters to find 'Mr. Right'"

An entrepreneur, her major asset is her voluptuous body. Her fault is not trusting herself when it comes to her personal life. She's conservative and finds it hard to let men into her world.

⸬ STORY THREE: KENYA

AGE: 29

CITY: Miami, FL

DATING STATUS: "Nearing 30 with the 'Can't Find a Husband' Blues"

Kenya, an investment banker, is running a battle against time. She's sexually uninhibited, loves the local South Beach scene and having drinks with the girls on Friday nights. But an affair with a Hispanic man changes everything.

STORY FOUR: ALEXIS

AGE: 25

CITY: Atlanta, GA

DATING STATUS: "Just out of a long relationship and looking to explore her 'other' side"

As a young executive, Alexis is tired of all work and no play. She's led a sheltered life but has a wild side to her. She loves the club scene, which leads her to new experiences.

STORY FIVE: WACEERA

AGE: 23

CITY: Chicago, IL

DATING STATUS: "Attached, but still out looking for the best man"

An avid traveler and assistant at a nonprofit agency, Waceera is bold with lots of choices. She's in a relationship, but she and her beau have "issues." Self-assured and assertive, she has one major problem: commitment.

STORY ONE

⁙

FARAH

24
BROOKLYN, NY

DATING STATUS:
*Caught up with some-
body else's catch*

THONGS, LAPTOPS, AND TOSSED SALADS

○○ I'm attractive and slender, wrapped in cinnamon brown
○○ skin, with long, "good" hair and an attitude to match the
assets. I graduated from the top educational institutions in the
country. I'm bright—a B. A. and M. A. degree in political science
from Columbia University and I'm a junior correspondent at *NBC
News*. I have plans to buy a few brownstones in Brooklyn and
basically kick some ass when it comes to making money!

Working at one of the nation's largest TV networks has its
perks: free admission to costly events, meeting influential people,
invites to all the right parties in the city, and mingling with politicians, officials, and the entertainment world. Like all jobs, it does
have its flip side. I'm one of two black people hired as correspondents, which makes it rather lonely. I've been here since college
and started as an intern. Though I'm a freelancer, I'm satisfied
with that. The freelancer's life is always full of adventure: What
will the next story be? Where is the next check coming from? As
a freelancer you carve your own path, and with the right contacts
you can basically live as good as a full-time worker—or better.

I've always been a writer, though. Before I could even write, I
was thinking. I had an imagination that would put Disney World
to shame! When I was five, a class assignment was to picture what
lives would we live as adults. Considering that as young kids we
could barely write a complete, coherent sentence, we had to "express" our thoughts and feelings. While everyone else wanted to

be some cartoon hero, I wanted to be a princess who lived in a castle on Mars, had servants, and conquered the universe. As I got older, I put my imagination into structured stories. In high school I was the assistant editor of the school newspaper, *The Times Observer*. As a sophomore, I uncovered a story where a senior was found out to be bribing a male teacher for an "A" before graduation. The senior, who was very popular, was expelled and the teacher suspended. Students loitered the hallways with newspapers claiming I had made the incident up as a way to get attention for my stories. I lost several friends and some officials refused to be used as sources for any of my future stories. But I got past that.

In college the stories were a bit more on the sexier side of things. The name of the college newspaper was *Ebony Voices*. You guessed it! It was the black student publication and I was editor of the relationships section, where I would get all the dirt on who was doing who and report it. A few relationships and egos were broken. Such as the boyfriend who was seeing another girl who lived right next door to his girlfriend in the same dorm. He would sneak out of his girlfriend's room and hide in the stairwell. When the coast was clear, he would knock on the other girl's door and be quickly let in. The "other girl" called in the story in hopes of finally breaking up his relationship. We promised to withhold her name, but we gave his name and the girlfriend's name. This was the biggest thing on campus since the boyfriend was the top point guard in his NCAA division. His girlfriend ended up dumping him and becoming friends with the "other girl." I guess in college people don't take certain things as seriously as we do in the real world.

Another incident involved a freshman having an affair with the dean of students. His name and full title were withheld, but the freshman gave detailed accounts of their times together, including the worn-down church shoes he would wear on every date. Since that article, all eyes were on administrators with church shoes! Instead of me being labeled a troublemaker, in college, I gained even more friends through my stories. Somehow everyone thought if they became friends with me, I wouldn't hang their ass out to dry. But if you put your business out in the street, someone is bound to sweep it up.

It was in college when I decided the school newspaper was just not enough. My professor introduced me to Lena, editor at the *Daily News,* who was a former student at Columbia. I was an intern there for a while but convinced them to let me write a story by the end of summer. It wasn't exactly Pulitzer-prize work but a small story on the fight to take back a community park. Finally, Lena let me do a piece on relationships between students and professors. The article included homosexual affairs, too. It did raise some eyebrows, but that time I blamed Lena. Anytime someone asked me why I included some private details, I would just shake my head and say, "My editor made me do it." The article was a hit and got me lots of local attention. I continued writing for the newspapers, as well as *Black Enterprise* magazine. I was lucky. This isn't usually the case with many young writers—black or white.

Landing the job at NBC was a godsend. Going from print to TV can make your head spin! Television is supersonic compared to print, where a lead time can be several months. When I told an editor I worked for about my television goals after graduation, she gave me the number of a "good friend" at NBC. The next week I was interviewing with Myra, and two weeks later I was traveling between New York and D.C. covering congressional/government issues and interviewing the bigwig policy makers and breakers. Anyone who's been to D.C. knows that the government can be very male dominated. Everywhere I went, there was a man I had to speak to, meet, or shake hands with. Most of them were grumpy, conservative old men, but many were young, aggressive, attractive, and on the road to success.

I don't have many capital affairs to share except one where I was covering a local party convention. On my way back from the vending machine after a long night of transcribing an interview, I walked past the half-opened door of an up-and-coming senator and his friends being entertained by several "ladies" in his hotel room. As soon as I made it down the hall to my room, the door slammed shut. Just earlier that evening the same senator had been campaigning with a doting wife and family standing at his side. There are always rumors of indiscretion in D.C., but I was more interested in making my own scandal than reporting others. Well, not a real scandal, but a private one.

When in town, meeting men in D.C. is not a problem. A lot of reporters stay in the same hotel for a few days when covering a story about a convention, meeting, or conference. At the end of the day when the interviews have finished, note taking has ceased, and keyboards have rested—it's time to head to the bar. The scene is like any other one, but this time the suits are lined with fat pockets. The same handsome reporter who ignored me in the hotel lobby is now trying to whisper sweet nothings in my ear;

the bar's patrons being policy makers who indirectly or directly have an effect on the laws and administration of this country doesn't make a bit of difference. It's just like when I'm in New York—*once a bar always a bar.*

THOUGH IT MAY SOUND like I'm doing pretty well, my Grandma Jesse always asks, "So when you gonna settle down and find you somebody nice?" My answer is, "I'm only twenty-four!" All I get is one of those, "These young people today . . ." looks. No matter how much I accomplish in my professional life, my personal life always gets the most scrutiny.

Working in TV news is constant work, unusual hours, and the schedule is unpredictable. One week you are working on the 5 P.M. show, and the next day you are doing the 4 A.M. show. All I wanted to do when I got home was sleep! Sadly, the men I'd be dating would think I was playing hard to get or cat-and-mouse games when really I just didn't have the energy. Some of them I really liked, but eventually they would disappear after a few weeks. I guess they have too many choices out there. But that was then and this is now. The career girl approach has landed me by myself too many nights. When the opportunity presents itself for me to have a good time, I'm there.

Still, there is the other issue of adjusting to what men want today. Men say they want a good woman, someone with goals, who takes care of herself. But when they see the hoochie mama with her breasts pouring out her shirt, their attention diverts to that and they completely lose interest in me. Or how about when I cook and try to get domestic, like I think some men appreciate, they want to be with the glamour queens and divas who think Pine-Sol is a new tanning lotion!

I'm a good woman who doesn't curse and has morals, but that doesn't excite the men I meet anymore. Playing by the rules sometimes lands me with the kit but not the caboodle.

IT'S THE BEGINNING OF my few days of vacation from work! No interviews, producers, or deadlines to meet. It's a Sunday night and I don't try to leave the house on Sundays, more less go to a club. But my girl, Lola, is really excited about going to Club Lotts on Spring Street. We heard it was off the hook on Sunday nights; and when we rolled past there Memorial Day weekend, we saw all kinds of people stepping out in everything from Jimmy Choos to Bakers, and from Range Rovers to Kias.

It was about thirty minutes before I had to meet Lola at the Bergen Street train station, and I just couldn't get myself looking right. I had on some tight, stretch, black pants; a strappy black tank top, and sandals. Since I was feeling really modest (being Sunday and all), I threw on a brown, long-sleeve sweater. And I even had on my work sandals. Flats! I swore when I first saw the place I would be in my tight Betsey Johnson dress, Dolce & Gabanna heels, skin glowing, and hair flowing. I was not out to meet anyone tonight but just to chill with my girl before she left for Baltimore on a business trip.

Once we got inside, it was like a scene from those well-known rap videos. Victorian couches, chandeliers, and mirrors adorned the room, and a long, wooden bar ran the length of the room upstairs. Everybody was posing, laid across a couch or sitting cross-legged on purple and red velvet sofas. With drinks in their hands, every once in a while someone would take a peek or glimpse at the sister or brother coming in. There were guys reaching over the bar buying girls drinks and scribbling numbers on yellow napkins.

It was a definite scene to be studied. Lola and I just sat on a couch and people watched for a while, listening to the sounds of De Angelo, R Kelly, and Mary J. Blige. When the DJ finally made it to the rap collection, people put their drinks down to get their dance on. Lola and I walked to the bathroom to touchup our hair and makeup, just in time to catch the end of Q-Tip's "Vivrant Thing."

Somehow we got caught up on the dance floor with the crowd. We could barely get halfway across the room! Lola and I just looked at each other and started dancing. After a few minutes, I lost Lola. There were more girls than guys on the floor, but at this point, the music was too good to be standing around. When Juvenile's "Back That Thang Up" came on . . . everybody went crazy. Suddenly everybody got a big ass they want to back up!

I managed to dance on the perimeter of the floor—so it can look like I'm dancing and standing (just in case anyone wanted to ask me, I could look available). Out of nowhere, I hear someone next to me yell, "OW, OW!" I turn around to see who had the audacity to complain about someone stepping on their shoes, which happens a thousand times in a crowded club.

"Excuse me, miss, but I just bought these Gators! How you

gonna do a brother like that and keep dancing?" He isn't the least bit serious. I notice the cutest smile across his lips, and he is supposed to be in pain.

I turn around and ignore him. About ten minutes pass, I'm about all backed up and feeling a bit tired. As I make my way through the crowd bumping shoulder after shoulder and being hit with drops of sweat from wanna-be Soul Train dancers, I walk to the bar for a drink. As I am waiting to get the bartender's attention, lo and behold, it's Gator man again.

He takes my sweaty hand, looks up, and begins counting one-by-one something invisible in the air. "I'm counting the angels up above because one of them *has to be* missing," he says, without a blink.

As I come out of the spell he put on me, I say, "That's a new one. So if I'm an angel, who are you? The devil?"

No answer. But Marcus' wit and bronze skin has me interested. For a moment, he just stares at me with those gorgeous, contrasting, light brown eyes, like I'm a plate of buffalo wings and a pitcher of cold lemonade with lemon bits.

He leans his six-foot-three, 230-pound, solid frame against the bar, as I press against him to make room for others trying to squeeze in. I looked around for Lola and saw that she had made herself right at home with a glass of red Alizé, laughing with some guy with dreads down his back. Her type.

"Tell me what do angels do to keep busy?" he asks with a cute, boyish smirk.

"Protect the good from evil," I say, as I turn around with my back against the bar. I felt his hot breath against my neck and his

Issey Miyake cologne whispering my name as he slowly straightened up and got the bartender to come our way.

He bought me a Tangerine Cosmopolitan and himself a Hennesey and Alizé. As I lick the corner of my lips to savor the Cosmo, I say, "I work at NBC during the day, but at night I'm fighting with the new laptop I bought. Are you into computers, by the way?"

"I'm especially into the HARD drive. The more bites and RAMS, the better," he says, with a sexy bedroom tone. I couldn't help but fall victim to his lines. His green Gators, Rolex watch, tailored pants, Caesar-cut hair, and hard, muscular body finally cracked open my defenses. And he knew it was working.

Lola finally walked over with the guy in the dreads. Marcus introduced the guy as his friend, Steve. It is a coincidence because Steve and Marcus look like total opposites. Marcus orders another round of drinks and pays for everyone's. We hurriedly sip the last of our drinks and head out to the dance floor as Sisqo's "Thong" starts playing.

Marcus wastes no time in trying to get to know my body better. *Thighs like what, what what . . .* As we dance, his hands are casually slipping and touching my breasts, which are bouncing against his chest. Usually, I would dance at least an arm's length away from a guy, if there's enough room, but tonight was different. Marcus feels my thighs when I turn my back to him and move my body against his already firm dick. It was a hot, summer night, and my mood was loosening up. Unfortunately, Lola had to catch a flight in the morning.

When the song ended, Marcus pulled me over to a corner as

we both tried to catch our breath. He wiped his wet forehead with the back of his hand and licked his thick lips. "Girl, you were shaking your body out there like you ain't got no mama!" He laughed. "When can I see you again?"

After I finish laughing like crazy at his country-ass remark, I say, "Just call me." I signal to Lola to give me a second. I take out a pen and I write my number on a napkin. I thought he would give me his, but he gives me his E-mail address. He tells me he just bought a computer, too, and wants to see if his E-mail works. I didn't give it a second thought. Usually I like giving guys my number first instead of me calling them. I leave him, standing with Steve near the steps to the basement lounge. I turned back to wave bye, but he was gone.

TWO DAYS AND COUNTING . . . my little vacation is dwindling. I have to cram everything I need to do in these last two days, including lunch with dear old mom. We meet for brunch at the Blue Note where Chaka Khan is doing her thing as only a woman named Chaka can. In between Chaka's soulful sounds being interrupted by applause, my mom and I share tidbits of information of the latest happenings.

"Did you hear that Nadeera's mother got her that job in the mayor's office as the press secretary's assistant?" my mom asks, with one eye on Chaka and the other on me.

"Nadeera? That girl barely finished college! I thought she was still working as a bank teller!" I say, totally surprised because Nadeera hated politics and only used newspapers for cleaning her windows!

"Evelyn called up some big guy there who gave the press secretary a glowing recommendation. Now I hear that Nadeera don't like the place," she says, looking through her purse for a mirror. "I have a feeling them people don't like her! Who can blame them," she huffs.

My mom never liked Nadeera after she swore Nadeera stole five hundred dollars from her wall unit last summer when she was waiting for me to come home from a meeting. Nadeera had been left in the house alone, but she denies it till this day.

Shaking her head, my mom admits, "Now you know she will probably be out of there in no time. But it's good to see a black woman can wield some power around this town to get her daughter in such a high-profile position." The old black couple, seated behind us, looked at us annoyed as we continued our conversation.

"Tell me about that politician guy you met a few days ago? You said his name was Marvin?" my mom says, as she looks up from her cappuccino.

She knew damn well I met some guy at a club, but it was her way of dropping her so-called subtle hints.

"No." I sigh. "I met a guy when I went out dancing with Lola the other night." Chaka is leaving the stage for a break. It seems like I missed the whole show talking to my mom.

"His name is Marcus. It's just a boy, no big deal. And before you ask, yes, I am keeping my eyes open for that young, black congressman from Indiana," I say, rolling my eyes and using my perfectly pink-polished nails to push my hair back.

"Oh, that's right, a club. That's nice," she mumbles, looking down at her cup. "But that Mr. Lewis, I saw him on *CNN* the other day, and it still looks like he has a naked ring finger." She leans forward, whispering like she doesn't want to spill the news. If I didn't know my mom better, I would think she had some political goals herself because she was always trying to hook me up with a politician. But what are mothers for! I've had my eye on Mr. Lewis, I mean Remington, too. But at first glance he can look a bit too stuffy and conservative.

Little did my mom know that I'd been through Remington already. We had a little fling when I was covering the recent Republican National Convention. He's not that bad in bed, and his conservative manner is only an act that he wears outside the bedroom.

At thirty-two, Remington was in the middle of his second term in Congress and was handpicked to speak at the convention. He's prestigious, well liked, and an advocate for Christian groups and antismoking campaigns.

It was my first major political event and he gave a hair-raising speech to the crowd of supporters. My producer, Sharon, felt that interviewing some politicians and gathering information for the senior correspondents was something a young reporter could handle. On my first day I was too overwhelmed. After his speech I was lucky to spot Remington surrounded by a small group of reporters who were holding on to his every word. I watched as the cameras flashed each time he raised his hands for emphasis. I was automatically drawn to him, and my insides got warm just thinking about what fucking a congressman would be like. It was a fantasy.

At a reception in a nearby hotel, we met as he introduced himself to the reporters in the room. When it was my turn, he held my hand a little longer than the others. I guess being one of the few young sisters there caught his attention in a room full of white-haired politicians. I was charmed by his stocky, six-foot-one frame and his perfectly trimmed mustache, which teased the lining of his curvy upper lip. The gentle clasp of his hand around mine told me he was charmed, too, by my "Tina Turner" legs. The rumor is he's quietly looking for a wife. I was twenty-three and just trying to finish my story. After the reception he invited me to an after-hours spot in D.C., and we exchanged phony conversation about politics, journalism, and success.

"Yeah, that would be great if that could happen!"

"You're right we need leaders we can trust."

"Politics used to be more about integrity."

After we skipped the bull and, of course, after a few glasses of wine, we let our true colors show.

"Damn, I love the way your bottom lip just curls," he said.

"You have such a firm butt!" I responded by grabbing it.

"What are you doing after this?" he asked, leaning into me. "Let's talk in the suite. I have some CDs we can listen to."

We didn't listen to CDs but made our own music. A total exhibitionist, Remington had a foot fetish and loved role-playing—especially bad girl, good cop. He loved my feet so much, he dipped them in all types of sauces he kept, along with chilled bottles of wine, in a small refrigerator near his bed. Strawberry, cherry, and orange sauces would trickle down my feet and toes as he savagely licked and sucked every drop! He was a tender lover, who liked women to take control. Tying him to the bed while I straddled his face was his special request.

Even now when we see each other, we give each other that "If they only knew" look and let our eyes do the talking. It was a one-night stand, but he's my ally now and in D.C. you can never have enough of those.

Mom and I watch the crowd begin to talk among themselves while they wait for Chaka and her band to return from the break.

"Mommy, Mr. Lewis is nice, but I hear he's courting some woman from his hometown. A family friend," I say, trying to hide the disappointment in my voice. I didn't like Remington like that because I didn't really know him. But it's not so bad to be the girlfriend of a popular politician and that hadn't happened.

"And you know, I just want a regular man." I signal the waitress to bring another cappuccino to the table. Running my fingers through my curly, light brown hair (something I do when I am nervous), I say, "Politicians travel too much. I want a hard-working man who can be there for me and not have me wondering all night where he is."

My mom hurriedly swallows her last piece of carrot cake and dabs her mouth with a napkin. Pointing at me, she gives me that "a man is a man" speech—again.

"I done told you these men are going to do what they want to! If you keep worrying about keeping some man home and knowing his whereabouts all the time, you are going to be alone and miserable."

She catches her breath. "A man is a man. You can't change that, just change how you respond to things."

My mom is a single woman. My dad was seeing her while he was married to another woman. My dad, William, was a horny little thing and produced a few more babies while he was separated from his wife. His wife never left. My mom still loves him and never utters a bad word against him. And his children outside his marriage adore him because we really don't see him. And since everybody else likes him, especially my mom, I never thought twice about things. Sometimes we all get together for Fourth of July picnics in my Aunt Lauryn's back yard in Queens—myself, him, his wife, and nine kids from his wife and three different women, including my mom. We all accepted that "a man is a man" and there was no time to harbor hard feelings.

Chaka's show is about to start again. As always she looks overwhelmed by her wild hair, but still fiery and sensual. Sitting back I adore Chaka's short, olive green chiffon dress that adorns her voluptuous figure. My mom and I sit quietly humming while Chaka sings "Through the Fire" and sway our heads to the beat, along with practically everyone in the audience. Another twenty minutes later and the show's over. Another sold-out performance. Now, true, I'm a little late into the game and don't know the same Chaka my mom knows, but good music is good music. Whether it's pop, rock, rap, reggae, world, or merengue, I listen to it all!

Though I love hanging with my mom, things can get a little overbearing at times. When she starts preaching, it's time to start leaving. That "a man is a man" talk always irritated me. We stand at the corner of Sixth Avenue and West Third to hail a cab. My mom waits on the sidewalk, against the periodic bursts of wind, while I try to stop a cab. It's loud, crowded, and every cab that is passing is "off duty" or full. *Damn! I hate this city. . . .*

"Baby, let me call Oliver, maybe he can pick us up," my mom says, waving me back in her direction.

Oliver is her "companion," both in their fifties and have been together for a few months. Oliver likes my mom because she always makes him feel like her rescuer and that is not my style. Just as I was about to turn back, a cab skidded to a stop right by my feet.

I bent over and asked "Seventy-second and Columbus?" He signaled for us to get in and my mom ran up to the cab in small, girlie steps. "This cab is filthy. I should have sat on a napkin or something," she says in disgust, holding her legs tight and close together. I sit back, spread out, and enjoy the ride.

"Baby, so tell me." My mom wipes a lock of hair from her face and moves closer. *Here she goes with her little whispers again.* "If you don't have a man, how do you get those *special* needs met? At your age you should at least have someone nice giving you some loving when you need it." She actually looks genuinely concerned.

Smiling reminiscently she continues, "Your mother has hung her coat up from her wild days. So my stories are old. And I know a beautiful girl like you has plenty. Now spill the beans because I know you got a potful!" she says, playfully nudging me.

My mom in her prime was basically a tramp! She'll tell you in a minute, too. Maybe that explains why she was so strict with me when I was in school. Now as a secretary in a law firm, she goes to work in her clothes from Henri Bendel, her designer hats, and her nose in the air. But she didn't get the nickname "Sapphire," after the beautiful stone, for just sitting at home. In the attic of our previous home, she kept a yellow shoe box full of photos of her and her friends in the '70s and '80s. Ms. High Society was posing with red leather minis, tight, coochie-cutter shorts, and revealing tops that poured out the ample breasts that I had inherited with gratefulness.

"Well, I have a friend who comes by on those cold nights. He's not too bright, a regular guy, lives with his mom, doesn't have much, but he makes up for all that with his size, tongue, and stamina." Unlike most of my friends, now that I am grown, my mom and I can kick back and talk about dick size and everything. She would eagerly listen because hearing my stories was like reliving her wild days all over again.

"You need those types around every now and then. Just use protection because we don't want you being nobody's baby mama. Oh, Lord, no!" she says, holding her forehead.

"I keep condoms everywhere in the house. I don't play that baby mama thing. Not cute at all. If he was a professional basketball player . . ." We burst out laughing, both knowing that I am too paranoid about protection to get knocked up by anyone—rich or poor.

The cab swings around Sixtieth Street and we hit some steep traffic. We may have caught up with those folks coming back to the city after the weekend. I look out the window, turn to my mom freshening her bright red lipstick. *I guess Oliver is home wait-*

ing for her. She has a natural beauty and needs very little makeup. Her smooth hair and skin always glisten and nicely frames her petite, but shapely body.

"These are the things we should discuss more often. Since you moved out, I feel we don't bond as we used to."

"I'm not trying to be rude, but my business is my business; and some things I like to keep private. When I was younger and in college, it didn't matter. I even followed some of your tips." My mom looks on with pride with that last one.

"But I like keeping some details to myself now," I say calmly, lightly touching her knee. I didn't want her to take it the wrong way because she had always lent an ear to me.

"I know. I was a little loose in my day. And I can see you have a little devil in you. Just knowing things sometimes just assures me that everything is okay. There are so many diseases out there now. When I was your age . . ."

"Okay, I understand what you're saying. And Mommy, no news is good news," I say reassuringly.

We remain in our own thoughts as we ride down Broadway to Seventy-second Street. It's warm, but the wind is making its own stand against the sun, making the day feel like it's 68° rather than 80°.

As we approach my mom's twenty-story building she says, "That congressmen we were talking about." She tilts her head with a sarcastic grin. "I know something happened when you two met. I know." Shaking her head, she continues, "You can give me the details next time."

How does she know these things? Before I could even respond, she opened the cab door to leave.

I look out the window while the cab is slowly driving away and say jokingly, "Next time we'll talk over pound cake and milk!" With a wave and a smile, she disappears behind the double glass door.

On the way to Brooklyn, the gentle whipping of my hair against my face put me in deep relaxation. I took a nap and dreamed of a tree and long blades of grass that turned into people. It's one of those meaningless dreams you get during brief naps. Just when the tree was about to start doing the macerena, I hear the cab-driver, with one of the largest moles I've ever seen on his lip say, "Hey! It's thirty dollars! Hello!"

I take away a dollar less for the tip because of his attitude. Running my fingers through my hair, I stumble to the front door. *My mom is tripping! She is probably out buying that pound cake now!*

All I want to do is throw on some Dinah Washington, run a cool bath, and slip into some comfy slippers. Then it hit me! I have to transcribe an interview I did with a Columbia University professor for a story package about generation X and political apathy! Though it's vacation, work never ceases. My boss always wonders why I spend time transcribing when we have assistants for that, but I feel I miss the tone and substance of a story if I just read a typewritten document. By the time I finish transcribing, I already know what I want to write and how to write it. It all unfolds in my head while I listen to the voice on the tape.

Max is waiting for me, knowing that tonight may be one of those all-nighters. Max, my old desktop computer, and I have been through it all, crashes, freezes, lost information. I grab some mango juice from the fridge, put my headphones on, and hand over a fine Sunday evening to my job again.

A half hour into my typing, the phone rings and practically hurls me from my huge, black, buckskin office chair. It was one of those earsplitting, powerful rings that usually signals drama.

"How you? Thought I'd give you a call before I head home," says Marcus in a husky voice.

"Whatsup! Are you driving?" I say, stopping the tape.

"Yeah," he says. "The song we danced to at the club is playing on the radio and I was having flashbacks of the way you were pumping your thing," he says, raising his voice over the loud music. Not exactly what I expected from our first telephone conversation.

"Don't think too hard, I don't want you causing any accidents. You should call me when you get home," I say, moving toward the window.

He gives an uncomfortable laugh and says, "I have a room-mate," his voice a bit unsteady.

"Is it Jack or Janet?" I ask, referring to *Three's Company*. There's a weird pause, and before he could muster up his answer, I already knew what it was. "Listen, just E-mail me when you can. I gotta go." Translation: Don't call back!

WEEK ONE

Saturday. I am wrestling with my new laptop, a granite iBook, and it is still giving me problems crashing and all that after a week. It's a sweltering Saturday afternoon and being patient with this machine is the last thing on my mind.

"Who's this?" I know damn well it is Marcus on the other line. I put down the troubleshooting guide and sit down. *Doesn't that man take a hint!*

"Whatsup!" he says, like it was the first time we ever spoke. "Steve wants your friend's number because he's gonna be in Baltimore for business soon and wants to say 'hi.'"

"I don't have it, and if she didn't give it to him, then she has her own reasons," I say firmly, but nice. I was relieved to get a break from the computer, and since our last conversation didn't turn him away, I wondered about his intentions.

"What are you doing in the house on a day like this?"

"Well, I told you about my computer. I'm trying to fix it now."

"Please," he says, laughing, "don't blow anything up!" I couldn't help but join in. I was close to throwing that computer out the window!

"What are you doing later? I may want to get you out of that house before you destroy something," he says, over the sounds of cars and horns on the highway. "Let me pick you up."

I look around my apartment, all the empty boxes, troubleshooting guides, the bomb message on my computer, then I look at the blue, wide skies, the warm air, and time of day. *Well, it may not hurt to hang out with him. He may make a good friend (especially if it is his treat).*

MARCUS CALLS ME ABOUT eight times before he gets to my house, for directions and to see if I am ready. I told him I would look out for him. He's driving a black Tahoe, which shouldn't be hard to notice.

Marcus pulls up about twenty minutes later. As I walk out my door, I try to picture his face in the club. I'm a bit nervous because meeting guys in a dark club and seeing them for the second time in light can be frightening. I hold my breath as I walk outside. He looks a little different but still a choice piece of man. I slide in the car slowly, making sure he sees the shape of my thighs in my jean capris. I look him in the eye and his light browns see right through me. All of a sudden I feel very small in his big car and not as confident. As we drive, out of nervousness, I start asking him lots of questions and playing with my hair.

He's an engineer at a large firm in the city, a dreamer, loves real estate, plays golf on the weekends, and plays with other things . . . women.

He then drops the bomb about twelve minutes after picking me up. "I live with my girl, who I've been with for years, and our six-month-old son. But I'm not satisfied, so I try to stay out of the house," he says, looking straight ahead as he drives.

Okay. Well, he's just a friend. No harm. After today, no more dates.

"Oh, okay. Yeah, everybody needs some time to clear their head," I say, trying to sound like a friend.

Getting all emotional was an option, but I decided to downplay his comment. At least he's honest, but it really didn't matter to me since I plan this to be the first and last meeting. Changing the subject to music and food, we drive around for about a half hour looking for a place to eat. We decide to go to Da Silvano in the West Village. In warm weather the doors of the restaurant open wide onto a busy sidewalk where we sit. He orders a tossed salad and Chicken Marsala and I have pasta with pesto and zucchini flowers.

During our meal, he talks a lot about himself, as if he was an open book. At thirty, he has a lot more stories than I do, especially about his time in the Marines. I tell him I love French food and am interested in Buddhism, something I recently began exploring.

"I don't know much about Buddhism, but I can cook you a nice French meal," he says, as he neatly cuts his chicken and bites a piece from his fork.

"And how do you plan to do that with a girl—and baby?"

He says, "When we're alone." We stay quiet about it, knowing that the idea is not too crazy. I stare at the small drop of gravy on his full bottom lip and watch as he takes his tongue out and licks the corner to get the lingering juices. Or was he showing me what he would do to me if we were alone?

I get up to go to the bathroom and I can feel the heat of his eyes examining the curve of my ass and the dip in my waist. When I return back, a few minutes later, I catch his eye. But he quickly turns away as if suddenly preoccupied by something in his pocket.

Him having a girl hadn't come up again since he'd mentioned it, but his smug look shows he thinks he's past that hurdle; it's time for a curve ball.

"So how does your girlfriend feel about you wandering off on warm, romantic evenings, leaving her alone?" I ask, playing with the straw in my cranberry juice.

Smiling, but looking downward as if hoping I'd buy the line that's coming, "She's too busy worrying about our son. Sometimes I don't even think she notices when I'm gone." When I look at him with raised eyebrows, he blurts out, "I'm serious!" *Maybe he is.*

"I know your girl can't be blind to the fact that many girls will be attracted to you. I find it hard to believe she doesn't care. Also, even the thought that your man could be spending your money on other women can make any woman start bugging!" I say, challenging him a little further. I lean forward and squint my eyes trying to understand.

Damn! He has the cutest dimples . . .

He grips his Becks Dark beer with his large, bronze hands, takes a guzzle, and pauses for the right words. "She has no idea what I'm up to." *Every woman knows.* "Plus, I am using my own money. Like I use my own money to pay all the bills, diapers, et cetera. I'm just trying to see what's out there again that can finally make me happy." *He's good at this stuff . . .*

"Like being with you right now makes me realize what I'm missing," he says, without the least bit of sexual innuendo.

As if he had a magic wand, the blonde-haired waitress interrupts our flow and leaves the check. *I had just a few more questions to ask but what the hell.* I make an attempt like I'm reaching for the check and he stops me.

Marcus grabs the check and says, "I think women should let men pay more often these days. You women always try to keep a man from doing his job," he says, as he digs in his worn, squash leather wallet, flashing several crisp hundreds.

"Okay." I smile playfully. "I'm not stopping you from doing your job as long as you spend a little overtime this way." I hold my hand out, while he looks on laughing.

. . .

LEAVING THE VILLAGE, WE drive to Battery Park and sit by the water. It was a bit too romantic for me and had me feeling a bit open—already. He's so damn funny and had me laughing all night at stories about his friends and family. *We're friends so we can talk about anything. Right?* He doesn't bring up his girlfriend. He doesn't make a sexual move on me the whole time.

We go back to the car and drive home in comfortable intervals of silence. It's nighttime, and in my neighborhood it gets so quiet you can hear the leaves rustling, the sounds of restless babies crying, and the clatter of dishes as folks conclude their evening dinners. We park in front of a dark house, which looks empty. Parking in front of just any house can provoke the owner to start peeking through windows.

"My girl is impossible," he says, as we sit in the car, no radio or music playing. "I shop for her, take care of the baby when she needs me to, and she's still not happy. I can't talk to her about anything because she's always tired or sleeping. Anything I buy her doesn't fit or it's not the right color. Anything I buy my son is wrong. It's like she doesn't even want me around."

How can a woman treat a man this nice so bad? He looks so sad. Poor thing. Another story of a brother trying to be good to his woman. BUT he was the one ready to cheat, not her.

"Well, why don't you leave if it's so bad? Take your son," I say boldly.

"I stay with her because I don't want to end up paying child support AND rent for my own place. I just need an escape. I don't think I love her. It's all about timing and making sure I got my shit right," he says, as he grips the steering wheel.

It's working. Believing that he has a girlfriend who doesn't care isn't so hard. It is possible. Maybe she doesn't want to be bothered since dealing with a baby is more than enough to handle. Or maybe Marcus is too much to handle.

Marcus pulls me up to my door and we both know things are a little different from how they started earlier in the day. I say, "Good night," and slowly get out of the car and come around to his side. For a few seconds I look at his eyes and those sexy lips and fantasize about kissing him. After I give him directions back to Connecticut, he waits till I get in . . . then he pulls off.

Damn! I wanted to kiss him. Oh, well, he has a girl.

He calls ten minutes later from the car. Refusing to play the good girl role and hide my feelings, I tell him I wanted to kiss him. He did, too. He tells me he's going to a bar on his way home and will call me later. *What kind of girlfriend is she? Doesn't she care where he is? Doesn't he want to be home with her? Why not?*

THE NEXT DAY, IT'S back to work. In a fast-paced newsroom, no one even notices when you leave on vacation except a few. I just always hate those, "So where you been? Out sick?" Can't a black person go on vacation! As I try to get my desk organized, Sharon comes by with that same crazed look in her eye. "Hi, sweetie! Good to have you back," she says. Before I can begin to utter a word, she continues, "Do you have that package ready? We'll also need a hard copy for the web site," she says hastily.

"Okay, I have a hard copy of the story," I say, handing it to her. "By the end of day, I'll sit down to edit the interview and pull some good sound bites. I'll have that ready by this afternoon. Then it's finally out of my hands," I say, a bit annoyed since this package has been looming over my head for a while.

"I see you're learning. In this business, you worry about your end of things. The rest will handle itself. Of course, if you're on air or live, then . . ." She starts getting on her "Journalism 101" speech.

"Then I'll still do my part because if one person is not doing their part, then that's a weak link in the chain!" I say, smiling sarcastically.

"Good, Farah. I like your style. You've learned not to take this place too seriously or you'll end up like me—insane!" she says, holding her hands to her forehead.

"Welcome back." She runs after a production assistant, her heels clicking down the hall, and shoves her a list of tapes to retrieve.

I spend the rest of my morning organizing my files and reading all the past issues of newspapers and magazines that piled up on my desk since I've been away. Just in case I missed anything. Marcus and I hung out pretty late last night, leaving me feeling a bit lazy today. Between flipping through the pages, my mind wanders to Marcus.

I never fucked anyone's—that I knew of—man before. Marcus is definitely a charmer just looking for a comfort zone. Or could it be he wants to live the vida loca *with a siren like me? Or to put it like Lola would, "That boy just wants some ass!"*

I get awakened by the sound of my phone ringing. "Ms. Hill speaking."

"What is up, girl! Sorry I haven't called since I've been back from Baltimore. I've been drained! What are you doing after work?" asks Lola, who sounds very excited. She definitely woke me up.

"Well, hello! I guess you have plans for us? What do you want to do?"

"Let's go to the Shark Bar. I gotta go, but meet me there at 6 P.M. Okay?"

Before I could even think, I say, "Sure." We hang up.

"YOU ALWAYS HAVE TO learn things your own way," says Lola, cutting a piece of fried fish. "I wonder how this one is going to end." She looks down at the plate like she's talking to the fish.

"It's just a friendly thing. He talks to me about his girl. He's not hiding it or playing games. He hasn't even made one sexual move on me," I say proudly. At the corner of my eye, I can see a young couple, where the girl is feeding the guy a piece of corn bread, then they giggle. Seeing happy couples together always sickens me since I can't even get a date for the company Christmas party!

The tables at the Shark Bar are really close, even a whisper can be heard by the next table. But this is something I wanted to keep quiet because Lola has a way of getting too loud about things.

"What he says now may be true at first light but a lie by noon," says Lola, lowering her voice.

She always had such flowery speech.

She continues, but this time a little less quietly, "Whatever you do, just make sure you do the fucking. Don't let him fuck *you!*" I took heed and the couple next to us made a face like they smelled something bad. *Uppity black folks . . .*

WEEK TWO

A few days pass and Marcus is on time. He called Wednesday morning to set things up for the weekend. If I can't have him for myself, and I don't want to take him away from his "little family," I can at least have fun with him. Plus, since he has such a passive girlfriend, there is no drama to hear of or that he wants me to know about.

I take him up on his invitation to go to Connecticut on Saturday. After the movies, we go to a small Brazilian restaurant where he knows the owner, a short, heavy guy. *Popular.* Marcus told me he and some friends had been going to buy it but had backed out of the deal because of disagreements over the direction of the restaurant. We sit at a table, located in the simple garden at the back of the restaurant. A petite Latina waitress with a swinging ponytail brings him a Beck's beer when we sit down. *He's obviously a regular here.* I order a Long Island Iced Tea to loosen up. Marcus still has a way of making me feel tense like he did that first time he picked me up in his car. We spend the evening giggling, flirting, acting silly. It was so carefree. I got a chance to escape from my hectic job, deadlines, and he got a chance to just sow his wild oats. I slipped out of my sandals with the skinny heels and played footsie with him under the table. He leaned back, slid down in his chair, and opened his legs wider. *What a dog.*

"Please don't let me stop you," he says, holding my calves. "You look innocent, but I bet you're a freak in bed," Marcus says, waiting for an answer.

"Some things have to remain a mystery," I say, taking my feet away and slowly sipping my iced tea. Curious, I ask, "What type of women do you like?" *I wonder how his girlfriend looks.* "Are you into thick women and big butts?"

Here come his dimples. "I like women, period. But I appreciate beauty over a fat ass. I see fat asses all the time. It's real beauty that's hard to come by," he says, with that smirk of his that says, *"Damn, I'm good at this shit."*

After he pays for the check—again—we leave. I get home about 11 P.M. He calls me ten minutes later—from the car.

WEEK THREE

Monday morning at work, Sharon calls me into her office. "Good morning. Just have a seat, dear. This won't take long," she says, getting up to close her office door. She's missing that crazed look in her eye, and I'm beginning to wonder if something is wrong. I have a seat and try to look as casual as possible.

"Well, you know you've been with us for a few years now, as an intern and now as a junior correspondent." She has a stern look that is examining my facial expression with her every word.

"Farah, the work you do is great. Especially for a girl so young. You're dedicated and can keep your poise and professionalism when things gets tough. Even under pressure, you always follow through." Smiling, she adds, "There's a full-time position opening and I want to give it to you, with a twelve-thousand-dollar raise."

My heart starts racing. A permanent position? Not exactly what I was hoping for. I'd take the raise, but I love the freelance life—the ability to take days off when I need it and to write for magazines and do stories for other networks.

"Wow," I say, my hand on my chest, "this is really unexpected." I hold Sharon's glance and notice she looks a bit disappointed by that fact that I didn't jump and say, "Yes."

"I've been freelancing for almost a year now and I enjoy it. However, I have thought about being permanent as well. Is it possible I can have some time to think about this transition?"

"Sure," she says, shrugging her shoulders, "take as long as you need. But I'm just telling you there are many freelancers waiting for an opportunity like this, and I can't hold out on them just waiting for you. How's a week?" Sharon was always the firm, to the point type, but always nice.

"That's fine. Or maybe even sooner. But can I ask one question?"

"Go ahead."

"Does the raise still stand if I choose to stay freelance?"

"The raise? My dear, I can't give you a twelve-thousand-dollar raise if you're not permanent. But your hard work can't go unnoticed. We can discuss a raise."

If I take the full-time slot, it will bring me to nearly sixty thousand dollars a year. But I would lose my flexibility. I can tell Sharon is disappointed. She is used to things going her way. But she also has a "motherlike" quality about her and I'm sure she understands that at my age it's variety that attracts me. Being tied down to a job somehow takes the fun and creativity out of things. I'll definitely go permanent in another two years, but television may not be where I want to stay.

"Well, I'll come back in a few days to discuss things. And, thanks, Sharon." I get up to go to the door.

"Farah," Sharon calls, "freelancers get sick and need benefits, sweety. Think about it. This is also a great opportunity to advance your career."

I smile and turn to leave. Sure, it can advance my career, but in this business the quickest way to advance is to go from job to job. Lately, I've been doing some print work, and I'm finding that interesting. I want to see what's out there—personally and professionally.

THOUGH MARCUS AND I are undoubtedly attracted to each other, we just have a plain, ole good time together. He's funny, witty, smart, attractive, and charismatic. If only men like him came in a pill, then I could put some in a potential, and unattached, boyfriend's drink! But I cannot say those things without reminding myself that he is also a cheating, conniving dog. *My mommy ain't raise no fool.*

We meet again the very next weekend and go see *Next Friday.* Throughout the movie, Marcus turns into an octopus, feeling my legs, breasts, and lips! I love every minute of it. As we laugh at the same parts, our knees and hands touching, I look around at the darkness of the theater. It's about 3:30 Saturday and it's practically empty. It's like our little retreat from the world because when the day ends, he has a girl waiting for him at home.

After we leave the movies, we drive around looking for what next to do. I told him we can do anything but that one "thing." He smiles. He knows what I'm talking about. In between deciding what to do, his car phone rings. *Could it be her checking up?* It's his cousin Chris, needing some money. So after a few minutes of all three of us deciding where to meet, we wait for Chris near a Bennigan's. Chris pulls up and Marcus gets out of the car to meet him. They laugh and do their "man talk" stuff before Marcus gives him the money. *Damn, the brother must be paid to be lending people money without a moment's notice.*

We go to a small restaurant just a few blocks from the Brazilian restaurant we'd gone to before, because he says "all the really nice places" are near his home. I tell him that I can't deal with all the restrictions in Connecticut and next time we'll be in the city. No response. We stay in Connecticut anyway and have drinks, dinner, and great conversation. We talk more about sex tonight than any other. Oh, may I add that before he came to pick me up, he told me he couldn't stay out past 9 P.M. Well, it's 9:15 now, and he hasn't even taken me home yet. Marcus is pushing for the hotel. We kiss across the table and flirt. I'm really feeling him now, BUT we leave and he takes me home.

All the excitement that built up over dinner had to be released somehow. On our way to Brooklyn, in the car, he starts rubbing my thighs and breasts, slow but firm. He unbuttons my jeans and slips his fingers beneath my red, stretch, bikini panties. He rubs my wet lips gently until I let out a soft purr. He slowly takes his right hand out while keeping his left hand steady on the steering wheel. He smells his fingers and inhales deeply like a hungry truck driver at a buffet. He then licks my wetness from his fingers and puts it in my mouth as I suck on it with gentle, pulling strokes. He's going like 60 mph with the moon roof up and trying his best to keep his concentration while he gives me pleasure. Cars are passing us by and big trucks, but we don't care. I lick around his ears with light strokes and work my way to his neck and unbutton his shirt, gently pulling the hairs on his chest with my teeth. He lets out a moan and sharply turns the car to the right accidentally. I sit up quickly, and we both give a weary sigh at the close call. He pulls up at two hotels . . . but it ain't happening THIS weekend. It's 10:30 P.M. now and we're lost. We ask for directions and find our way back onto the highway and go back to doing what got us lost in the first place.

Once near my house, we sit in the car for a few minutes and kiss. He begs me to let him in my apartment, but I say no because it would be bringing him further into my life. We realize it's after 11 P.M. and call it a night. Home by 9? Not tonight. He calls me a few minutes later on his cell phone.

WEEK FOUR

During the week, I speak to him several times. One night I decide I want to give it to him. Tired of waiting and rationalizing shit. This time I'm going to do something because I want to without driving myself crazy thinking about it. And you know, I didn't even rack my mind because I am sure this is what I want to do. I'll wait till he calls me later to tell him.

AFTER LUNCH, I STOP by Sharon's desk. She's hoovering down Chinese takeout. I turn to leave, but she calls me back in.

"No, no, it's okay, come in!" She wipes her mouth with a napkin and closes the lid on her food.

"What's up?" she asks.

"Sharon, I like it here a lot." I sit down with my arms folded. "But I can't go permanent now. Eventually I will, but I like the flexibility being freelance gives me," I say, feeling I'm doing the right thing.

"I just want you to be happy. If being freelance does it for you, fine. I certainly don't want to make you go perm and have your performance start to decline," she says, rolling up the sleeves of her pink, chiffon blouse. "But this is the only permanent slot I have for now. I don't know when I'll have another one; the longer you wait, the more competitive it becomes."

"I do want to wait for a bit and I'm willing to take that chance. People have come and gone since I've been here, I know what it takes and I have it."

"Good, that's what I want to hear. Just let me know when you think you're ready, and we'll do something about it," she says happily. "And don't worry about the raise." She winks and starts to finish her lunch.

Boy, was I relieved. I thought she was going to put on the guilt trip. Or force me to take permanent or leave. I guess, I just realized how good I have it here. If it ain't broke, don't fix it.

· · ·

A MESSAGE FROM MARCUS greets me when I get home, as well as lilacs left on my doorstep. *Lilacs?* If he knew he was getting sex next time, would he have done this?

I go into the kitchen and put them in a vase.

"THANK YOU SO MUCH!" I say into the phone when he picks up.

"Well, I'm just that type of a man." Confidence is something Marcus does not lack.

"Look, I have something to say."

Silence.

"It has nothing to do with the flowers at all! But last night I decided I want to give *it* to you," I say, in a low, sexy voice.

He knew the time was coming.

"Keep in mind, I don't want any ten-dollar motels."

"I'll get some nice shit. A hotel. Don't worry about it, I'll take care of it. You just worry about getting yourself ready," he says.

"*Also,* since I don't bother you about living with your girlfriend, I want *all night* instead of a few hours," I say, with a firmness that surprised him.

He sighs—several times. "That's gonna raise questions. That's something I have to build up to with explanations. I can't just do that. What time exactly? I have to think about it," he babbles.

I told him to think about it, but that is the only way he was gonna get some.

The next morning at the office, while I'm reading the paper, Marcus calls me the earliest he ever has. "You're not being fair," he says, with a whining tone.

My body twists in my chair. He may be right. I did go into this situation knowing he had a woman, knowing he had restrictions.

Why make this difficult? . . . What am I trying to prove?

I've done the worst thing already—seeing a man who lives with his woman and baby. I let him explain his case.

Losing some leverage, I say, "Okay, we'll work something out. Maybe it doesn't have to be all night. But it isn't going to be pick me up early and have me home by midnight either." We had a deal.

FRIDAY. I LEFT WORK early after a press conference at City Hall. I know what tonight means, and there's lots of work to be done. There will be lots of scrubbing, exfoliating, shaving, primping, and clipping before Marcus and I meet later. While I'm waiting for my toenail polish to dry, he calls me about 3 P.M. asking me what time could we meet. When he finally picks me up, I am too tense and unusually quiet! And now that I told him what he was getting, he is expecting nothing less. He talks nonstop on our way to Connecticut, while I listen. He doesn't want to go the movies AND dinner. He says that it would take up too much time. Instead, he takes me to the nicest restaurant he has yet. A seafood restaurant right by the water. We eat crabs, fish, and mussels, and order a bottle of white wine. Boy, did I need that wine! During dinner we talked about fertility, gambling, books, and babies.

"What would you do if you got pregnant now?" he asks. Not exactly something that makes for a good dinner conversation.

"I'll keep it. I'm old enough and working. Plus, salmon enhances a woman's fertility. So if you are not careful tonight, you might be in trouble in about nine months," I say, waving my fork at him.

We both gave a nervous laugh and moved on to other topics. After dinner, I go to the bathroom. When I get back to the table, I see Marcus has already paid for the bill and is waiting for me by the exit. He wastes no time!

My pager goes off during our drive down the highway. Marcus looks over with a look that says nothing is getting in the way of his plans tonight.

It's a page from a source I've been trying to reach for days. It's 9 P.M. on a Saturday! There is no way I am calling back since I wouldn't be able to do the interview now anyway. I turn my pager off.

Most of the drive was silent, with a few snippets of laughs here and there as we listen and talk about the music that's playing. We know what's next, but we have to be cool about it. *Oh, I know what we can do, let's get a room.* That was his attitude, and I liked it. We go to the Grand Hyatt. We get there a little before 10 P.M. He was dying to get this, and the day had finally arrived. His consistent pounding on weekends and phone calls and money spending has finally payed off! And I, finally, get to do what I want: be a little bad and have a little fun.

After his shower, he comes to the bed with a white towel wrapped around his waist. It's off in a microsecond. I still have my skirt and clothes on because I like it when a man takes off my clothes. It makes me feel sexy, desirable. He unbuttons my skirt and pulls my blouse over my head. He lays me on my back and pulls my panties to the side and begins licking my pussy in featherlike strokes. In between licks, he looks up and talks dirty to me. I arch my back and wrap my legs around his neck. He opens my legs wider and I gasp. Finally, my warm wetness flows down, and he licks it up like a cat licks milk.

I lay there and try to catch my breath. He rises up and gently rubs the head of his dick against me. He teases me until I practically beg him to put it in. My thighs flex and relax around his waist. But I'm not gonna let him do the fucking. I get right on top and ride him like a racehorse. Our eyes lock, without blinking, and he looks so vulnerable. I just want him to grab my hips and say, "I want you! I'm leaving her and taking the baby and coming to you!"

I lay over him and kiss his forehead, lips, neck, and smear my breasts across his chest. I kiss down to his stomach, to his belly button, and to the hair between his legs. I tilt my head and lick his dick and his balls. Breathing full and hot, I eclipse his dick in my mouth. I raise and lower my face over his dick and steady it with my lips and tongue pressing against it. He looks up at the ceiling and in his words . . . "What are you doing to me?" "Shit!" "Ohhhh, damn!"

His hands go over the small of my back and pull and tug on my hair. Ears, lobes, neck, nape, all get touched so passionately by his lips. I wiggle my way from underneath him and go the extra mile. Never having done this before, I close my eyes, hold my breath, and stick my tongue in his ass. He yells. I want every part of him. *Everything.* I couldn't stop. *We could be so good together.* All the feelings I had been holding in since we'd met just started pouring out. *I wish he were mine.* After a few orgasms, we run out of condoms. He wants to go raw. *Hell, no.* That's where it stops. He falls asleep a few minutes later, resting his head on my stomach. I watch *Saturday Night Live.* At about 3 A.M, we get dressed and leave.

I'm relieved when I finally get home. Back to reality. I can't wait to go to sleep to dream a better ending to this night. It's already happening; I'm falling for him. I wait for him to call from his cell phone like he usually does, but he doesn't. Maybe because it is late (after 3 A.M.) and he knows I'm tired. Or maybe this is where things are about to change.

Marcus calls me the next day. We don't talk much about it. But he tells me his dick is sore and he thinks I broke it. *There he goes being funny again.* He was just joking, but I know I went to work on him last night.

For a few days I experience some really nasty discharge, serious latex burns, and vagina swelling. I'm not that nervous yet. I usually have adverse reactions to latex condoms, especially once I get dry and don't lubricate enough. Maybe I was paying too much attention to making him remember me that I forgot about *me.* But after several days of discharge and itching, the thought that I may have caught an STD crosses my mind.

After work, while sitting in the library doing some research for a story I'm working on for *Black Enterprise* magazine, I lose my concentration for the third time. *Maybe that's why he wanted to do it raw. Maybe he has something he was trying to pass on. Why else would he want to do it raw with someone he hasn't known that long? How many women has he done it raw with?*

I call my gyn and get an emergency appointment the same day. As I wait in the patient area, I begin thinking of all the ways he could have given me something. Just when my eyes begin to water as I picture every possibility, the nurse calls my name. The doctor gives me the whole gamut of STD tests. I have to wait for the results, but the doctor says from what he sees I have nothing wrong with me. Everything looks fine.

I page Marcus when I get in and tell him I just got back from my gyn. He asks me how everything went (he doesn't know why I went). I tell him that it was just a routine exam. Later I find out that the tests were all negative and all the swelling came from having recently shaved my vagina. The prickly hairs were irritating it, causing me to itch, and the discharge was normal but just aggravated by the conditions. I must be paranoid. It's Friday and we still haven't made plans to see each other this weekend. *Damn, by Wednesday he usually made sure we had plans for the weekend.* More shit had done changed. Okay, I'll play it cool. He asks me what I'm doing for the weekend, and I ask him the same. Still no plans.

WEEK FIVE

It's Saturday, 2:30 P.M., and I still haven't heard from Marcus. *Fuck that playing cool shit. I want to see him.* I call his cell and consider the risks since he could be with his girl.

"Whatsup," he says, in his usual casual way.

"Can you talk?" This is the standard question every time I call him. Just in case.

"Yeah, it's cool. I'm at the mall."

"What are you doing later? Because a friend of mine wants to hang out [a lie] and I want to know if you were coming out to Brooklyn," I ask, hoping he can make it. It was a pretty desperate attempt, but he has me hooked.

"I'm shopping with my goddaughter," he says. "I'll call you back about 4 P.M. when I'm done. You know how you women like taking all day just to buy a T-shirt," he says, as I hear him paying the cashier.

He calls me back at 4 P.M. on the nose, as he promised. He is going to a party a friend is throwing, who also happens to play for the Nets. He asks me if I want to go. *No thanks.* He had told me about this party a few weeks ago, and it had finally arrived. Damn, I'm disappointed. Seeing him every Saturday for a month kind of had me open and spoiled: driving around in a nice car, going places.

Okay, it's just one weekend. The man just probably wants a little break to hang out with his friends. No harm done.

He still didn't make any plans for Sunday.

Thinking about the last weekend had me wanting and expecting more this weekend.

Sunday night I made plans to go to Lola's barbecue party. I haven't seen Lola since the Shark Bar, and we've been playing phone tag for the last few weeks. But I need to see him, too. I page him and tell him I want to see "Woody" tonight. He calls me back right away. He's on his way to a meeting with a contractor and will be out by 10 P.M. We make plans to meet at a building in Soho later on.

When I reach Lola's neighborhood, I immediately feel lost. I'm not too familiar with Bed Stuy or which direction to walk. I stop at a corner where the bus leaves me and approach a group of guys in head kerchiefs and T-shirts standing in front of a bodega. I saw them eyeing me since I got off the bus. These guys look a little shady, but they are still men. And if you approach them with a smile and in a respectable manner, they are like anyone else. I ask the one holding the pit bull for directions. After a few flirtatious comments from his friends, he points in the opposite direction.

I walk up to Lola's mother's redbrick, three-family house. A child opens the door, and I walk into a plethora of voices and the smells of fried chicken, macaroni and cheese, and barbecue.

"Now you want to act like you know somebody!" Lola says, hugging me at the front door. "Look at you, your nose is as wide open by this food as you are by Marcus!" she says, grinning.

"SHHHH! And I can't get enough of both," I hiss.

I go into the living room and greet her mother, aunts, and uncles. It was my first time meeting them, and thank God my time was limited. I go to the back yard where Amel, Lisa, Silas, and Maurice are sitting. Silas is who I call on every once in a while for sex, but no one knows. We give each other a secret embrace with our eyes. I walk around and give everybody a hug, except Silas, since we weren't supposed to be "that cool."

"Damn, I wish I could stay, but I have to go meet a friend."
Silas pretends to ignore me.

"Here you go again. Why didn't you just bring him?" asks Lisa,
twisting her short fro.

"Well, it's not that easy," I say, looking at Lola, who knew exactly what I meant. I turn to Silas, who looks away, letting the
light reflect off his bald head. Silas and I have been over. But there
are still some unresolved feelings. I basically used him for sex, and
he started liking me and I didn't have the time.

"But I am definitely fixing a plate before I leave." I turn to go
to the kitchen and Lola follows me.

I sit down in the kitchen at the small, checkered cloth table
and update her about Marcus.

"Do your thang. But the ball will drop, and it may fall on your
head!" Lola warns me.

I didn't want to get Lola started, so after my meal, I left.

I took the A to the 1 train and used the time to think about
what exactly I was doing. Across from me was a black lady with
jerry curls, wearing a canary-colored shirt, jeans, and sparkly pink
toenails, while a white man, in khakis and a blue shirt, sits to my
left reading the business section of the *New York Times*—not looking up once to see what his stop is, like he innately knows. *I
wonder how I lost my leverage and put Marcus in control.* If this was
the old me, I'd be home right now making hot cocoa and getting
ready for bed.

The worst part about seeing someone else's man is, I can't even
see him when I want. When Marcus' schedule allows or when he

can get away is the only time. I do feel him moving farther away from me. *Maybe he is starting to sense that I'm getting attached?* My thoughts get interrupted by a dumpy white woman with glasses who plops down right next to me. She's obviously a tourist, looking around clueless like an elephant on the Brooklyn Bridge. Tourists in this city are obvious! They keep their eyes plastered, watching each passing stop and momentarily get up thinking it's their stop only to run back in the train and get caught between the doors. *Damn, I need a car. . . .*

I get to the building, a little past 9:30 P.M. and don't see him. After ten minutes, I see khakis, T-shirt, and Tims walking toward me with a swagger.

Holding my hand, he says, "We'll leave in a few, but I got to let some people know." He holds me by the waist and grips a handful of my ass. He asks, "You want to come up with me and say hi?"

I'm the shy type and tell him I'll wait in the car. But after some convincing, I give in. Marcus introduces me to his coworkers, while he says his good-byes. He had to know this would make me feel good. *He introduced me to people.* For a few moments I am not someone he is trying to hide in his life.

On our way to Connecticut. He reminds me of our conversation over the phone earlier. *Damn, what did I start now?*

"Can we see a movie before we go get a room?" I ask.

"Look, there's no time for all that. You said you wanted to see 'Woody' not a movie," he reminds me.

We finally decide to just get a room. It's not the Grand Hyatt.

"Last weekend an old friend who knows my girl said he saw my car. I'm not going through that again," he complains.

What a weak excuse. He's not the only one who owns a Tahoe in the Northeast. So we get into a little something about that. He says it gets him mad when I don't trust him. *HAH! Let's not go there!* Anyway, he convinces me to go a motel. Going to a motel was something I was trying to avoid, but we are both tired of driving around. He suggests several motels and we settle on one. Then it begins to dawn on me how familiar he is with these places. Finally, we drive up to a motel, he goes to the desk and reserves a room. As we go upstairs and open the door, the first thing I notice are the mirrors on the wall he had mentioned. *Is he a regular at these places?*

As he usually does, Marcus takes a shower. The whole motel thing was a slight turn on and picturing him in the shower had me anxious. Feeling a little sneaky, I walk over and peek inside and see him soaping his body. I walk into the tub and surprise him. I run my slippery hands down between his cheeks and find his balls dangling low. Leaning forward, I lick the tip of his dick and trace my tongue around the head. I lick slowly up and down the shaft, showing him my skills as the water beats against my face. When he tells me he's about to come, I stop. He turns the shower off and carries me to the bed and starts kissing, sucking, and nibbling on my breasts.

"I'm doing the fucking this time. Just lay back. I'm in control now," he says, looking down at me.

I just closed my eyes and he disappeared into my body. Holding his ass, I just imagine how good it would be to get this every night, instead of every once in a while like I'm used to. It was kind of good to be submissive and let somebody else do all the work for our satisfaction. But of course, I did my little tongue tricks in those dark places.

We got our clothes together and left the sweat-soaked sheets and my fantasies behind.

"Come on," he says, rather aggressively holding the door while I walk out the room.

"Don't you mean, come on, please?" I say, making fun of his tone.

"I know how you like it. 'Get your ass out here,' is more to your taste." He smiles.

As we stop at the bottom of the steps, we hit the vending machine up. Good sex always brings on the munchies. We get some juices, chips, and cookies and just sit on the steps and talk. Sitting there, we laugh at the sounds coming out of the room next door and wonder if that was how we sounded. The rain was coming down hard outside and sounded like it would get worse. We went outside under the pouring rain and calmly walked to the car. Somehow, running to keep ourselves dry, was not on our minds. With Marcus' jacket around me, we stopped, dripping wet, in front of his car. He gave me one last kiss, until all the curls in my hair were straight.

WEEK SIX

I took some days off from work to clear my mind about this Marcus situation. The next day he didn't call nor the day after. Now I was really thinking about needing this. Mainly because how I felt when he dropped me home the other night, and I just don't want him to break it off first. It has to end sometime. I'm starting to feel a little guilty about the whole thing, scared of getting hurt and knowing what comes around eventually goes around. *Why am I with him—another woman's man?* He still goes home to her every night, she still cooks, cleans, and washes his dirty drawers; and she gets the money. I am worth more than a Saturday or Sunday dining and sexing. I know I can have a brother who has the money and the car and he can be *all* mine.

IT TOOK THREE MONTHS for him to call me again. Since then we talked every few months, if that much. We still talk off and on. But we haven't had sex in seven months. The last time we saw each other was during a weekend in September. But no sex. We just got together for a game of pool and a few drinks.

"I want to see if I can find another girl to be the third in this threesome I want to do," he says, as he looks at me intensely.

It was then that I was reminded that Marcus is just one of those guys who have an itch to scratch, and once he's done, he'll go back to playing "the good man."

"Uhm, well, I'm not prepared for all that." *What the hell is he talking about? Is there some crack in that beer he's drinking?*

I continue, "Three's a crowd. Plus, you and I need to finish our business before we get others involved," I say.

He just laughs it off.

"What kind of business?" He leans closer and stretches his hand underneath the table. His fingers dance between my legs until he slips one inside me. This is easy considering I had on a short sundress. This is definitely a good way to change the subject! The young Asian waitress knew what was happening the whole time. Every time she passed our table, she would give Marcus these wistful glances. I guess Asian girls have a little freak in them, too!

I had really missed Marcus. While at the restaurant he says, "I'm leaving town next weekend. I'll be staying at a coworker's house in the Hamptons. We'll have enough time to do whatever we want then—just you and me."

"That is almost too good to be true. But I have a cousin's baby shower to go to and a few other things. I'll call you by Friday and let you know," I say, as I munch on my last shrimp.

"Oh, okay. Just let me know," he says, nonchalantly finishing his beer, which later I found out meant that my ass was cut out the moment I told him I had something else to do. When I did call him that Friday, it seemed that he had made other plans.

I was just tired of the whole thing. It had been almost a year since we had had sex. *What were we still doing?* He made promises to see me, but never did. Actually, it had ended the last time we had sex, I just never knew till the last minute because I was waiting for more, when more was never coming.

Marcus in my life really changed my view on men and dating. It has become more realistic. I do not regret being with him. I learned a lot about myself and about men's indiscretions. In the beginning I thought I'd never date a man with children, more less one who had a girlfriend. Trying to be someone I'm not cost me a whole lot of precious time that could have been spent with someone who was made for me and not for someone else. This was a relationship, though bad, a guilty pleasure with a lesson. The lesson read: Get your own man!

STORY TWO

⠿

ALAYA

26

SAN FRANCISCO, CA

DATING STATUS:
*Carefully treading the
dating waters to find
"Mr. Right"*

LEGS CROSSED, HEART TANGLED, MIND CONFUSED

○○ "You can play the drums on that ass, gurl." "You can make
○○ a man cry with that onion!" my perverted Uncle Joe used
to say. Every day on my way home from school I'd pass by him
and his drunken friends playing dominoes. Anytime I hang with
my less-endowed girlfriends, the attention diverts to me. It is usually positive but sometimes downright annoying or offensive.
Shopping is usually the worst experience I would go through for
the week. When my smaller friends can bounce into a store and
grab a size six or eight pants and skip right out, I have to try
everything on, find out about return policies, and half the time
the pants can't get past my hips. I can make the classiest outfits
look pornographic or cheap because my ass stretches everything
out of place. At the office, you can find me in loose-fitting blouses
or jackets that go over my butt. I don't tuck shirts in at all! It's a
love-hate thing.

My friend Angela is tall, slim, with long hair, with a barely
there ass and always gets more white-collar brothers. I pull men
wherever I go. I get them all—the white-collar ones down to the
street peddlers. But men always have this assumption about me
that I am a freak. Woe to the man who makes that mistake! I am
a "tight ass with the big ass," my sister, Inga, calls me sometimes.
I'm one of those girls who brothers may call stingy. I like to hold
out as long as possible when it comes to sex. One-night stands
and "experimenting" is not my thing. Don't get me wrong. I can

handle my own in the bedroom, tabletop, wherever, but just can't seem to pin down a guy long enough to get there.

My younger sister, Inga, is a stripper and my brother, Umar, joined the air force years ago, and I haven't seen him in months. After graduating from San Francisco State University, I fell in love with the city's life, vibrancy, and tranquillity. The tales of the gold rush, the smell of saltwater in the air, and the prospect of being hit by an earthquake that can make any day your last left me enamored.

It is a sharp difference from growing up in the Detroit projects, where we all literally lived on top of each other and your business was everybody else's. Leaving Detroit to go to SFSU was a blessing. If I had stayed, I'd probably be on my second child by my third baby daddy. A year after graduation, earning my certification and becoming a CPA, opened new possibilities. Armed with the three Bs—beauty, brains, and booty—left me with few friends, and the few I did have were always jealous or insecure around me. There is something about a sister like me, five foot ten, with a high ass, long, slim legs, and a small waist that can make any woman look like "Olive Oyl"—frail and pale in comparison.

OPENING AN ACCOUNTING FIRM with Fernando, a Spanish gay guy from my previous job, has given me a new confidence and keeps me busy on those horny, cold nights. Fernando is in charge of all the numbers, and I make the sales calls to attract new business.

"Honey, use what you have to get us some more clients. You meet with men ninety-eight-percent of the time. Throw away

those steel power suits that make your shoulders look like a quar-
terback's. Soften up, switch those hips, and show off that ass. If
you don't, I will!" Fernando would say, moving his hands fast,
every time I would come back from a new business meeting with
no contract.

"We don't want you mixing business with pleasure, Fernando.
I don't know how those male clients can resist you in a skirt," I
would say sarcastically.

One day I had an appointment with Strooker Campbell Meyers, a law firm that had opened in the area. I was meeting with
Peter Strooker and Jeffrey Meyers, both salt-and-peppered haired,
white males in their fifties. I wore a fitted, floral, knee-length
skirt, trimmed with soft ruffles, and a twin sweater set with a
sexy V-neckline. My new approach landed them as clients the
same day.

Instead of us celebrating together, Fernando left early to meet
"he's so cute" for dinner.

"Who are you going out with tonight?" I ask.

"Oh, he's so cute! You have to meet him one day. We're going
to Emily's for drinks," he says, as his eyes shoot from the clock
back to me.

I want to celebrate, too, but I don't have anyone to celebrate with.

"Go by yourself," Fernando urges. "Beautiful women alone are
mysterious and appealing to men. It's the ugly, fat ones who look
lonely. Do your thing, girl. You won't be alone for long." I look
up from the copies of the signed contracts to respond, but Fernando was already out the door.

LATER THAT EVENING

Vivid is in the downtown San Francisco area—a club I've been to a few times and feel really comfortable at. It is close to the train station, just in case I have to leave alone. I'm all dressed up with fitted boot-cut pants that show the curves in my legs and hug my ass. Black, strappy shoes, a low-cut, red tank top and a loose-fitting gray blouse—don't want to overdue it.

Getting to Vivid early means catching the free buffet of buffalo wings and curly fries. But I'm late. I walk in about 8 P.M. and am engulfed by the latest hits and the sound of men's laughter and women's giggles. I check my blue cashmere coat, quickly make my way to the bar, and buy a drink to keep my hands busy. I reach over past the couple next to me and grab a handful of peanuts and crackers and watch a rerun of the De La Hoya and Trinidad fight. Leaning against the bar, I glance at my watch a few times to appear like I'm waiting for someone. Jay Z's latest fills the room as I take a quick sip of my martini and see people charging towards the dance floor. This scene is all too familiar. It doesn't have the same excitement it used to have when I was twenty-two or twenty-three. At twenty-six I can tell the silver from the platinum, and the Rolexes from the fifteen-dollar look-a-likes you can buy on the street corner. But unlike most people, I feel you can find that special someone in a club.

It's a good thing I came alone because there are a few guys watching my every move. This makes me a bit nervous, and I spill my martini on the bar table.

"Let me get you another one of those," says the stocky bartender, wearing a tight muscle shirt as he whips up another concoction before I can even look up.

"Don't worry about it. It's on me. I see somebody has got you waiting, so I figured I'd be the nice guy."

A free drink. Now that's the language I speak. "Thanks. These guys have me feeling like I'm under a microscope." I take extra napkins, just in case I get clumsy again.

"Well, when brothers see a nice woman by herself, it's like a dog around raw meat. Give it a few minutes, and it'll tear it up. I guarantee you one of those guys will be here any minute." At least I know I am not paranoid and imagining things. He turns his head quickly to take an anxious patron's order. When I look up after checking my watch for the twenty-third time, I catch a brother's stare. *Now this one is not too bad.* About six foot one, 190, blue-black, Gucci shoes, bald head, and skin the color of pancake syrup.

Midway through my second martini, I notice that the brother had finished his drink and might be feeling a little ambitious. I get comfortable in my chair and catch Trinidad giving De La Hoya a serious beating. I could care less about this fight, but looking interested keeps me busy. I look in the direction where that brother was standing, but he's not there. If he wants to get to know me, he'll come to me. Women these days may be getting more aggressive, approaching brothers first, but men should always feel like they chose you. I look up at the bartender and see him smiling and shaking his head, while he blends Cosmopolitans for the two women sitting next to me. The next thing I know,

POOF! that guy appears. He almost threw me off my seat! Okay, maybe it was the martini.

"Daaayum, you look goooood," he utters, resting his eyes on my hips. He shakes his head and wakes up from his four-second fantasy.

"I'm Keith and your name must be . . ."

"Alaya," I say, shaking his hand. I stand up from the bar stool, adjust my blouse, and give him a chance to savor the menu. Looking over his shoulder, I see the bartender giving me one of those "I told you so" looks.

"Seems like your martini is done, baby. Want another one?" he asks, taking out his wallet and calling the bartender.

"No, thanks. That was my *second* drink. I do want to be able to stand up," I say. By now my face is feeling tight and itchy like it usually does when I am a bit drunk. He grabs a stool and pulls up between me and another group of girls, who are giving me really nasty looks at this point. He orders a gin and juice, and I blurt out, "I know it looks like I am by myself, but I was with a friend who got an emergency beep, then . . ."

"Okay, calm down. It's okay. I'm glad she's gone. Now I can have you to myself." He pulls my chair closer to him.

"Actually, I'm here celebrating my first client. I just opened a small accounting firm with a friend."

"That's cool. You doing your own thing. Too many of us are happy with just a job. I'm a brother trying to get mine, too," he says, with a tone that shows me he's not only charming but confident.

"I'm a stockbroker at G. P. Stanley, so I make myself and people lots of money—to put it simply. Hopefully, I can show you how to invest your time. I'll take care of the money," he says, with a broad smile showing off impeccable teeth.

Keith puts his drink down and gently pushes back a strand of hair from my short, feathery cut. His hand accidentally brushes my hard nipples. Noticing his contact, we both let it go. He wasn't actually that close to me, but I haven't been touched by a man since Clinton was in the White House. My nipples may have been greeting him. It was purely innocent.

He tells me he just got back from Cincinnati, where he was helping his father campaign for city councilman. Now I'm impressed. He's smart, paid, family-oriented, and actually gets along with his father!

I ask him what he is thinking during a few minutes of silence over crab cakes and the bottle of merlot he ordered. Keith says, calmly, "Eating you."

All I could do was laugh. He laughs, too. My eyes and curiosity widen at his honesty. We both are drunk and our inhibitions gone. I know some nasty thoughts are going through his mind when he's just staring at me. Though what he said isn't the most romantic thing, I just felt like hearing it. I haven't dated in over a year. And it's only recently that I've been following Fernando's advice of loosening up a bit.

We spend the next half hour talking about life and relationships.

"Women don't know what they want today, especially sisters. They don't know what a good man is, and when they find one they are always suspicious."

"Well, I always believe people are suspicious when given a reason to be. However, I see your point." I try to keep my answers short, so I can see where this brother is coming from.

"I've been single for almost a year and a half! I've dated plenty during that time. And always seem to end up with, 'Ms. Insecure,' 'Ms. Materialistic,' 'Ms. Neurosis,' 'Ms. Suspicious,' and the infamous, 'Ms. Tie the Knot.'"

"And I guess you were the innocent little lamb," I say, laughing, but at the same time wondering which one I could be.

"I'm not perfect, but I know what I don't want." He pours himself another glass of wine.

I suppose this is his way of giving me the subtle warning. But we are similar in the sense of our frustrations. We both are successful and just want simple relationships with normal people, and not with those who have multiple personalities or games up their sleeves. And I'm not perfect either. God knows, I have issues I am struggling with.

As the dance floor and bar get more crowded and the voices get louder, Keith suggests that we go up to the lounge and "relax." Holding his hand, we dip and dive through weaves, stiletto heels, bump the big Prada and Fendi bags, and step on a few Italian leathers. In the lounge we find a comfy, green velvet couch across the room and around the corner from two white girls and a black girl smoking cigars. The room is dark with lots of nooks, so we have our privacy.

We sit back on the couch, and I stretch my long legs out over his lap. *"Ms. Materialistic," "Ms. Neurosis," "Ms. Tie the Knot"* keep resonating in my head. He must have caught me wondering.

"I hope what I said down there didn't turn you off," he says, matter of factly. Like if it did, it was my problem.

"No, I'm just wondering what you may call me. But honestly, I have a few categories of my own that I've met." Now the liquor is really talking!

Looking interested he asks me to name a few.

"I don't know where to start there are so many!" I named them all by something outstanding about themselves or character. "Baby mother man," "Lexus Man," "Blimpie Man," "Music Man," "Hundred-Thousand-Dollar Man," "Freak Nig—"

"Before you go on, how the hell did my man, Mr. Blimpie, get his name?" he asks, filling my glass with the last bit of merlot.

"He and I had made plans to have lunch one day. He asked me first. I agreed and he met me outside my office building during lunch. Thinking we would go to a nice, reasonably priced diner—at the least—or the trendy French bistro—at the best—we ended up at a dingy Blimpies! He didn't even pay for my turkey sandwich! Now that was no class," I say, disgusted at the recollection.

"True, I would have at least paid for your sandwich," he says, massaging my legs. But we both knew that a brother like him would have taken me to the French bistro.

Keith and I are just clicking. We're talking like friends but touching each other like soon-to-be lovers. I can already tell he is a great masseur. *Hopefully he can substitute for Alex (my Jamaican massage therapist) while Alex is in Napa Valley attending a seminar. I wonder if Keith can give a good foot massage? Definitely need that before my next pedicure. . . .*

"Girl, where is your mind at? I know my massages have a certain affect on a woman's concentration."

I remain silent, but smile. I doubt he wants to hear about Alex or toenail polish.

The truth is, I am feeling very relaxed with Keith. And if he is going to be around, a pedicure—really soon—is in order! My body tends to, let's just say, stay very natural when I am not dating.

He leans over and I feel the warmth of his breath against my ear. His fingertips brush the tips of my hard nipples (this time on purpose) poking out through my red tank top. Keith practically has me taking my nipple out so he can take a "quick lick." I thought about it until a few more people trickled into the lounge. We just lay across each other, dangling our glasses of wine. Our thoughts were silent, but our eyes were doing all the speaking. There was a nice feel in the air between us that our meeting may lead to positive things. I liked his confidence, assurity, and directness. He liked my smile, agreeable manner, and—my ass! I'm just being realistic about things.

We leave Vivid and quickly walk down the street to catch a cab. He offers to pay my cab home to Noe Valley. He lives in Embarcadero and walks to work most of the time. He gives me thirty dollars for a twenty-dollar cab ride. At first I was a little taken aback, but maybe it included the tip. I thought it was a nice gesture and I liked him for being concerned for my safety. When I got home, I heard his message on the machine, some gibberish about hoping I got home safely.

. . .

I CALL HIM BACK a few days later, and we make plans to meet Saturday. I want to take it slow since we were practically on our third date the first night we met. Just as I am thinking about changing from my short, fringe skirt to my jeans, he honks his horn.

My mother always told me never respond to a man honking his horn outside your door. He should walk up to your door like a gentleman and knock. But these days, figuring how fast men come and go out of my life, that just wasn't applicable anymore. I didn't want every guy I met to see my apartment.

I grab my snake-print clutch, get a bit frazzled, and misplace my keys. I look everywhere and can't find them. *Oh, gosh, if I can't find these keys . . .*

I open the door, and with my index finger, ask him to wait one minute. I turn around to run upstairs and see my keys lying on the end table near the steps. I guess with my nervousness I was probably looking right at them and didn't realize it.

I'm just going to leave before I find something else I never lost. Seeing Keith again has me wondering if he thinks I'm a cheap bimbo. I was quite flirtatious, open, and maybe a bit too friendly when we met. I hope he doesn't think I'm an easy trick or something.

I walk outside and see him adjusting things in the trunk of his beautiful, silver BMW 740i.

He turns around with a smile and before even saying hi, he says, "I was just keeping myself busy since a minute really means twenty," closing the trunk.

"Sorry. I just got a last-minute phone call." Can't give away that I was actually sweating bullets inside.

He opens the door on the passenger side and I step in. He starts the car while looking at my brown, shiny legs. He leans over and pecks me on the forehead and says, "You look delicious." I thank him, trying to hide my blushing face.

In the car our conversation is light but a bit stiff, considering how close for comfort we were when we met. We both were trying to be on our best behavior.

"That night we met was a lot of fun," he says, glancing over at me. "I never got that close to any girl I met the first time."

"It was a first for me, too. I guess I was feeling good and all with getting my first client. And the martini helped," I said chuckling.

"Oh, so are you saying that I had nothing to do with you getting so turned on?" he asks.

"Sure you did. But I really was just in a good mood. If it was another night, I may have called the police!" I say jokingly. But it seemed like I was the only one laughing; Keith didn't find the police thing all that funny.

"There you go, talking about calling the police on a brother who is just trying to get to know a sister. A consenting sister," he adds.

"I did give you the green light. What can I say! It was the way you touched my skin that drove me crazy!" He laughs because that was exactly what he wanted to hear.

As we drive downtown, he abruptly says, "I'm hungry. I may

stop at a restaurant and get a bite." He makes a right turn to a local takeout.

"I'm not that hungry now," I volunteered. I am a bit annoyed. *What if I was hungry? Why did he just want to get something for just himself? And a takeout joint out of all places?*

We get out of the car and walk inside and join a line of screaming kids and impatient customers. He orders chicken and broccoli and we sit at a grimy booth. I was pissed off at this. I don't eat Chinese food, nor do I consider eating at a takeout spot a good first date.

"Look, I know you may be a bit annoyed with us stopping here, but I didn't really plan the date out and didn't plan to take you out, out. I just wanted to hang out," he says, wiping the grease from his lips. Hang out?

Could this be one of his tests? I know Keith is definitely not the cheap type, but he was acting like the no-class type today. Since it was our first date, I was just going to lie back and observe.

After he eats, we drive along and stumble on an outdoor play at a nearby park. It was an African-themed play about a Nigerian chief who is split between his ethnic group and his government. Unfortunately, throughout the play, Keith talks nonstop about the costumes.

"Now that's a hot design right there!" he says, pointing to one of the actors playing the older son. "My man just got married and wore one of those in his wedding."

"It's called an *Agbada,*" I say, annoyed.

"Yeah, yeah," he says, "something like that." He obviously didn't pick up my tone and wraps his arm around my shoulders as we watch the play. It was quite funny at some scenes, and Keith and I laughed in unison, and I practically forgot about the Chinese takeout fiasco.

There was a small crowd of mostly couples sitting and enjoying the play in a breezy fall afternoon. The background was a sky the shade of cerulean, regal, aged trees, and a wide lake with a few rowboats going nowhere. It's times like this when I wish I had a boyfriend I could just snuggle up with or catch a quickie behind a tree with. But here I am on a don't-know-if-I-like-you-yet-so-don't-stand-too-close-first date.

I wait for intermission to use the bathroom. I excuse myself, walk past Keith, and he says to my ass, "Look at that wagon you are dragging."

People turn around to look at him, and I walk right by them. It's obvious this brother says whatever is on his mind, and I want to be ready to react to what he sends my way. But today I wasn't in the mood.

The play ended to a standing ovation. Keith took it upon himself to talk to the actors to find out where they got their clothing. *How about where they got the idea for the play?* I just stand to the side and wait impatiently. He comes back with flyers and information about their other performances in the city. It was kind of cool because I never would have known they had several other plays going on if Keith hadn't approached them. He's not what I'm used to and a bit unorganized, but he's interesting. And interesting can be good once in a while.

It's late, so after the play we decide to head home. During our conversation in the car, I found out several things about Keith, including his taste in women. Keith has seen it all and admits to seeing an attractive woman every fifteen seconds on the streets. It's the ones who try hard to look good who are a turnoff to him: the cheap skirts, the cheap shoes, the heavy makeup, the borrowed styles, the attitudes, the overdone hair, and the fake nails.

"Those women are average. All they are looking for is attention. They're cute and may be sexy, but you forget all about them when the next hot chick starts walking up the block. None of them stand out," complains Keith.

He says he's attracted to a woman's fluidity, uniqueness, and the quirkiness that makes her special. It's the casual, unassuming stance that he likes, the femininity and the mystery that makes him remember.

"That's what I liked about you. When I saw you spill that drink at Vivid that was straight up clumsiness. It showed you were a little fidgety because of all the attention. It was cute," he says, dropping me off at my door. "Whereas some girls would have walked all around showing their ass to everyone—and you *do* have a gorgeous ass—you didn't do that. I knew you were different," he says, convinced.

THE VERY NEXT DAY when Keith calls, he admits, "I know we got off to a rocky start yesterday, but I still had a good time. You have this certain quality about you that I'm attracted to. I knew you were upset about the takeout thing, but you held it together like a real lady."

I was so surprised because I was sure that my displeasure had turned him off. "Yeah, well, I just was trying to go with the flow." What I really felt like saying was that I had already made my mind up about him at that point. But by the end of our date yesterday, I'd started to like Keith. I liked the way he thought and was glad that he'd called.

"I must know. What the heck made you stop at a takeout joint? Were you like testing me?" I ask.

"Like, maybe," he says, mimicking me. "Well, I wouldn't say it was a test, but I needed to figure you out before I started taking you to five-star spots." He paused thoughtfully. "I see you're an old-fashioned girl. You are a limited edition these days."

Then he drops the inevitable, "So why don't you have a man?"

Damn! I guess I put my foot in my mouth. I hate that question because it is the same question I ask myself a hundred times over. I am still trying to figure that one out. I'm twenty-six and haven't had a serious relationship in three years. I refuse to succumb to sleeping with someone else's man, lowering my standards, or becoming what these girls today call on "independent woman." That leads to all the wrong things—overworked, unappreciated, and lonely. Though I've tried to avoid it, I've been sucked in. I have it all, but that one relationship with a man to make me happy. I once read that a woman without a man is like a barren field without seeds. A man is that seed, the seed that will cover the field with flowers. And if that's the case, my field is drying up!

"That's by choice. I'm just taking my time until I meet that right person." Whoa. What a generic answer. I wonder if he read right through that one.

"You're trying to tell me, you have a hard time meeting men

with how you look? Are you sure it's not about you being scared or trusting yourself when you meet that right person?"

This brother was deep! He hit it on the head. It's been awhile since I had this type of conversation with anyone. He was right, but he didn't have to know all that.

"I'm still trying to figure things out. But another thing is that brothers don't know what to do with a sister like me. Even before the sex, they have some kind of performance anxiety. I am smart, attractive, possess a nice body, am successful, ladylike, polite, and nurturing. They just don't know how to juggle everything. The common excuse is: I'm not good enough for you."

After a period of comfortable silence, Keith says, "I can relate to that. Sisters see me single, with money, attractive, aggressive, very flirtatious, with a bad-boy edge, and they immediately think I have some kind of script I go by to get them on their backs. Sex these days is being given away. That's not always the objective." I hear him in the background adjusting the phone cord. "But sometimes it is when the sister is showing a superficial side of herself, then I show a superficial side of myself."

I flinched when he said that. Obviously, he is very observant of women and their actions. It made me feel like he was watching my every move. But I am still not convinced that he doesn't have some game or some objective. He just has too many things going for him, he has to have several women pursuing him or meeting his needs.

"You seem to know it all, Keith," I say sarcastically. "I would really like to meet some of those women you've been dating and see what they have to say about *you*."

"It doesn't matter what they think. I know you and I have a lot in common. We're both two frustrated people who want to find that right person, minus the confusion. Talking like this really helps me see what you're about. How's dinner Wednesday after work?"

Now he's talking. "Cool. Would you mind picking the restaurant and letting me know?" He agreed. This is my way of testing whether he knew his stuff.

A FEW DAYS LATER

Fernando and I spend most of Wednesday morning organizing files of new clients and preparing some promotional packets to mail out. We're trying to line up enough clients before tax season, and it's going pretty well. It's a two-person office and we can't handle more than forty clients and we're practically there. While I listen to Fernando go on and on about "he's so cute" (I still don't know his name), the phone rings.

"Hey, baby, whatsup?" says Keith.

Off guard I ask, "Hi, who is this?" holding the phone closer. I knew it was Keith, but he can't call me at work like I'm at home.

"It's me." He sounds disappointed like I should have known.

"I know it's you. But this is where I work. I don't always pick up the phone you know," I say, a bit annoyed by his lack of office etiquette.

"Relax, I know your voice by now." He's a bit confused at my reaction but continues, "I was doing some research and found a good place on Mission Street."

Researching?

"Pintxos. It's a nice Spanish restaurant with a decent wine list."

"That sounds good," I say, feeling a little guilty. "It's usually hard to just walk into Pintxos and get a seat quickly. I'll make reservations for us now." He agreed. I made the reservations in his last name.

After work, Keith meets me downstairs. We drive to Pintxos, which is about twenty minutes away. While we stand outside the restaurant looking at the menu, I'm surprised at how expensive it is.

"Forget about the prices." He shrugs, noticing the expression on my face. "I like to dine expensively sometimes," he says, holding my hand as we walk in the restaurant to be seated.

Keith and I giggle trying to find what to eat among the confusing Spanish titles. We sit back and talk over glasses of chilled sherry. We order the house-made gazpacho, paella, and tarts for dessert. We then order a bottle of their finest sherry and spend two hours, eating and talking away. Finally, the check comes. It's almost $100 and he leaves a generous tip. Class, too. We leave and walk down busy Mission Street holdings hands. This date is definitely better. I like him now. . . . a lot. He seems more relaxed and organized. Everything is going smoothly. There was no way I was going to let this one slip through my hands.

THREE WEEKS LATER

I am really falling for Keith. I am absorbing everything he says, does, and thinks. He's sincere, insightful, and even though we got off on the fast track, he didn't make any assumptions about me. He's always treated me with respect. He seems confident, secure, and has this manly "I'll take care of it" attitude. I love that. But why is he single? Sure, he said he has had problems with women, but there are plenty of women like me looking for "the one." Why can't he meet those? What is he really looking for?

After almost a month of seeing each other, I know the issue of sex is bound to come up. We've kissed, hugged, but we've never been alone. We've been going out every weekend, and he drives me home but doesn't come inside. It could be that I haven't invited him in. I've never been to his house either. I know I am not ready for sex; there is something telling me to hold off on it.

During lunch, I tell Fernando about Keith for the first time.

"Girl, he sounds like a catch! He's calling all the time, lives alone, nice car, no kids, and is interesting! You have to bag that!" he says excitedly. He actually sounded more excited than me.

"I don't know. I like him, but I still have my antennas up. I don't know if he is Mr. Right," I say, playing in my grilled-chicken caesar salad.

"Alaya, you are always second-guessing yourself. You're the type of woman who will have lots of 'what-ifs' if you don't start living life. Mr. Right or Mr. Right, now what's the difference? Just try having a little fun."

"Fernando, I have a plan. I'm not wasting my time like these girls out here do, running into relationships ass first and then it's over in a few months. I want to take my time, feel things out," I say, reaching for the french fries.

"I'm not saying rush anything. But you are waiting for your Prince Charming. Sometimes you may come across a frog who can

then become your prince," warns Fernando. "Girl, we are all waiting for our knight in shining armor, but those days are over."

Deep down what he said hurt. I still want to believe that perfect
man will come into my life. I'll just bump into him unexpectedly
one day, and we'll find out so many things we have in common.
He'll be tired of the dating game and want to settle down. Family,
good friends, and good food will keep him happy. An old-fashioned
type of man. We'll be open and honest with each other, discuss our
goals, and totally balance each other's lives. I'll have three kids, be
the wife of a successful businessman, take vacations, and go sailing
on the weekends.

Fernando disturbs my daydream. "What about sex, have you
done that yet?" he inquires. "Oh, excuse me, I should know better," he says, rolling his eyes and finishing off his vegetable soup.

"Sex? Oh, please, I still need to know what he eats for breakfast! It's only been a month."

"You need some good dick to release all that tension you're
holding in," suggests Fernando, who's always been genuinely concerned about my lack of a sex life.

"Maybe." *I wish he would mind his own damn business.*

"And another thing," says Fernando, as he starts packing away
his leftovers, "be suspicious about those successful, good-looking
men with no women. They usually have small dicks."

"What? Fernando, that is the stupidest thing I've heard you say
today."

"Look, honey, men like Keith make money and can have any
woman they want. They usually ask for someone successful like

themselves and on their level. But when they get it, they become all insecure because they know sooner or later she will see his thumb-size friend. So instead, they commit to an average girl with no brains because she makes him feel good about his small dick. When really those kind of girls are just in it for the money. But a smart sister like you, who has her own, does not need to put up and shut up—with any man."

I could not stop laughing at his little theory. "Well, I don't know how big his dick is, but I've often wondered why he is so available."

"Hmmmm. Just see for yourself." He turns around before leaving. "But at your stage, big or small . . ."

"Yeah, yeah, I know, but I want more than just sex," I say, breaking him off midsentence.

WHY PEOPLE ALWAYS THINK I'm uptight, I don't really know. It could be that I'm the antithesis to my sister, Inga. Inga is bold, a risk taker, just as pretty and sexy, but overtly sexual and secure in her own body. She's also insecure in things where I am confident and struggles with her relationships with men like I do. We are shaped differently; and if you look at us, you'd think I should have been the stripper! Inga is more petite and her goods are in a smaller package, but she knows how to work it. She's been living in Virginia with her baby daddy for the last few years. I don't talk much with her at all. Anytime we talk, it always feels forced or fake. I never really feel like she's being honest, she always complains that I'm too stuffy and shows pangs of jealousy. When I went to college, Inga went to work. When she got kicked out of the house for stealing money, her baby daddy introduced her to stripping. Ever since then she's become a completely different person. She's looks ten years older than her twenty-three years, has marks from fights with other girls, and is just worn down mentally. Maybe it's seeing what overindulgence and materialism can do to you that has made me who I am. I don't take too many risks unless I'm sure about something and walk the tightrope, I've seen where you land when you fall.

That evening I go home to my quiet apartment, my lovable cat, and my messy bedroom. I have one message on my machine, Keith. I think about the conversation with Fernando earlier. The part about Keith being a good catch keeps ringing in my ears. I am trying to be careful not to get hurt or waste time. *Am I being too careful?* There I go questioning myself again! But I refuse to give up my fairy-tale fantasy. My match has to be out there somewhere. I believe love finds you, you don't have to look for it, grab it, or steal it. But there is an unevenness about Keith that I just can't put my finger on.

I straighten up the room and get ready to do the laundry. But I just can't get my body to cooperate with my brain. I am feeling quite depressed. Even though I don't have any friends, there are some girls that I used to hang with in college who are either engaged or married by now. At the very least, they are in a relationship. I have nothing! Just the beginning of something that is so new I can't even call the person and tell them how I really feel. There's nothing worse than starting out with someone. You don't want to call too much. You don't want to tell them your problems. You don't want to seem overanxious. It's just so fraudulent because you don't get to know the real person until three or four months down the line.

I stroll into the kitchen in my favorite bunny slippers and calmly fix a tuna sandwich. Then I sit in front of the TV and watch *Who Wants to Be a Millionaire*. I could call Keith and invite him over? Maybe that would be too forward. Plus, if he wanted to be alone together, he would have invited me over to his place weeks ago. Looking at the broken light fixture over the living room, it would be nice to have a man around sometime.

I reach for the phone to call him back but decide to wait until I get ready for bed. If I do it now, I may end up with him here and I'm not ready to go there.

THE CRASH OF A small plate on the floor wakes me up! My cat knocked over my plate on the table and it shattered to pieces. It's almost 11:30 P.M. and I must have dozed off. After scolding her, I grab the broom and sweep up the pieces of glass. Then the phone rings.

"Hi," I say, relieved to hear Keith's voice on the line. It felt like I was in a bad dream the whole time before the phone rang.

"Did you get my message about calling me back? I had wanted to go for a little drive tonight. You know, just chill, relax," he says, waiting for an answer.

"I was going to call back, but I dozed off accidentally," I said, putting the glass in the garbage.

"Okay, well, I know it's late. Get some rest, there's always another time." He hangs up.

I thought about it and realized that the dozing off excuse was bad. It put him in the "unimportant" category and raised the question as to why I couldn't call him before falling asleep.

THE NEXT MORNING I call Keith before I leave for work. It's early but it'll show he's on my mind and maybe make up for missing him last night. I invite him to a party Fernando is throwing for several of our new clients. It is at Club 369, near Gore Park. When I invited him, it took little convincing, he was ready to be part of my world. I'm sure he was relieved to know that I am opening up a bit. Meeting coworkers is a big step because once people see you with one guy, they always keep referring back to that same one no matter how many years have passed.

Friday night Keith picks me up on time, as usual. I am wearing a sophisticated, black, chiffon halter dress with tiny polka dots and silk tie scarf, and he looks sharp in all black—shiny leather blazer, slacks, and turtleneck. After I introduced him to a few people, we take advantage of the open bar. Over a few Coronas for him, and a few Cosmos for me, we get cozy in a nice empty corner, reminiscent of when we first met. Kissing, rubbing, whispering, we don't care who is watching us. Fernando walks over with Alex, the infamous "he's so cute."

"Fernando, this is Keith . . ." Before I could even finish introducing them, Fernando blurts out, "This girl you have here is a special thing. They don't make 'em like this anymore," he says, playfully showcasing my body and face. Laughing, Keith gets up and shakes Fernando's hand. "I just wish I could get her to give a brother a chance, let a brother in," he says, looking at me the whole time. "Nice to meet you, Alex," I say, shaking his hand. Alex was extremely shy and reserved and stayed to the side.

"I feel like I know you already. Did anyone ever mention how good you two look together?" Fernando asks. He looks Keith and me up and down and shakes his head. "A match made in heaven!" he says, clasping his hands together.

Annoyed, that's how I feel now. Hitting Fernando's head with the heel of my Via Spiga's is next. I pull him by his Armani jacket and take him to the side. Keith stays behind, looking a bit confused since everything seemed so funny to him. But Fernando was pissy drunk. I don't want Keith to think I've been bragging about him all day at the office, which I do sometimes. He can't think he has it that easy!

"Boy, what is wrong with you?" I say to Fernando, with his back against the pay phone.

"There you go again! Lighten up, chica," he says, taking a gulp of champagne from his flute. "That man is sexy. Look at those broad shoulders and those teeth! RRRRRRR . . . I'll tear him up!" he says, joking around.

"Well, he is mine tonight. And it was too obvious what you were doing out there. I don't want to make Keith feel uncomfortable. You practically have us walking down the aisle!" I say, pointing to the table where we were sitting.

"Look, I didn't want to get you all upset. Anyway, it seemed like he was enjoying it to me," he says, rolling his eyes. "You better go attend to him, the vultures are hovering nearby," he says, pointing to two very attractive black girls, one with a tattoo on her belly button, smiling at Keith, who was smiling back.

"See what you did!" I playfully push Fernando, and I walk back to the table. As soon as I sat down next to him, the girls diverted their attention somewhere else. Fernando and Alex hit the upstairs lounge. I guess Fernando felt he had started enough trouble for the night.

"So I see you were being entertained while I was talking to my friend," I say, a bit jealous.

He shrugs. "You were not talking but obviously arguing with Fernando over something so minor. He seemed like he was just having some fun with you," he says, shaking his head.

"I know. He just gets carried away sometimes. But you were all teeth with that girl over there."

"If you leave your meat out in the street, a dog will snatch it away," he professes. "Anyway, she was just flirting with about every guy in here, including me. Those are the types I may smile at, but I never take it further." And I believed him.

All of a sudden, feeling a little bold, I expose the string of my black, sheer thongs and play with them. It always take a drink or two to invigorate me. As I stand before him, he pulls me close and nestles his face between my thighs and inhales. He tells me, pressing his mouth between my legs, "I just want to swallow you whole until you melt." My heart races.

Just when things start getting good, a few club patrons walk into our little area. "Sorry, looks like you guys were having a little party of your own. Sorry if we interrupted anything," an Asian woman in her thirties with a little blue dress and bright red hair says, as she and her friends sit right next to us.

"Oh, no problem. We're newlyweds. We can't keep our hands

off each other," Keith lies, as he adjusts his pants and pulls me closer to him. The women smile and look away a little embarrassed. After a few minutes, they forget we are even there, and Keith and I get back into our little world.

I sit on his lap, as we talk about taking a trip to Saint Barts this summer, and our career plans for the future.

"I'm just doing my own business thing now. But it's still like a job. It's still something I must do every day to make a profit. But once I make some money and a few smart investments, I'll feel a lot better. Then, if I get married, I can stay home with my kids and leave the work world behind." I didn't want to mention the word "marriage" to a new guy since that is a major faux pas in dating books, but it slipped out.

"That is refreshing to hear," he says, pulling me to him. "I don't think most women think like that anymore. They are many unhappy women wishing they could do that and have a man provide for them." He continues, "I would want my wife to stay home, just like my mom did with us. That's why now I am busting my ass at thirty-three to make sure by next year things are straight," he says, as he guzzles down the last drop of his beer.

Times flies by and it's about 2:30 A.M. when I look at my watch. Keith wants to go back to his place. I want to go so bad, but it's too soon. It's only been a month. He tells me how we can make love and have breakfast in the morning. But no . . . too soon . . . I don't want to mess things up. He suggests us going to dinner. Where some guys would have given up, he wanted to make the night last.

We left and a found a nice café for dessert and a bottle of

Pelligrino. There was enough alcohol in our systems! Instead of sitting across from me, he sits next to me and constantly plants warm kisses on my cheeks and shoulders. He asks me to go home with him again. I say no. But I really want to! *Why does he want to move so fast?* He drives me home and we kiss good night.

WE SPEAK THE NEXT day and he tells me he dreamed about me the night before. "It was a purely sexual dream, but it came from all that pent-up energy I had. But in the dream, I just couldn't keep you. It was weird like that."

"I had the same dream! It was sexual, too. I guess you weren't the only horny one last night," I say. But really my dream was more on a romantic scale with us being together like a couple.

We make plans for the coming weekend to go to the museum to see this photo exhibit on Cuba, which the *Examiner* had given rave reviews about. At the museum, he is all over me. We are practically tripping on each other's feet because we are walking so close. I suggest going to his house after the museum. He seems really surprised like I'd caught him unprepared. But he agrees, and warns me. "It may be in a little disarray."

On our way from the museum to dinner, we share plans for the following weekend.

"So what do you have planned for July Fourth weekend? Because last year my friends and I went to Martha's Vineyard, but I don't know if I will go again this year. I think it's a place to go with your boyfriend not a bunch of girls," I say, hinting that maybe we can do something together.

"My ex's birthday is next weekend. I know it may sound

weird," he says, as he turns the corner to the restaurant, "but she doesn't have any friends or family here, and she is very depressed and under clinical care. So I told her I would spend her birthday with her to keep her company."

What! Where did this mysterious ex come from?

"So what do you two plan to do?"

"She wants me to spend the night, keep her company. We are *only friends*. It's just she has serious problems, and I feel somewhat responsible for her because I am part of the reason she moved to San Francisco years ago. It's really nothing. We don't have sex, if that is what you are getting at," he said, with a slight bit of annoyance in his tone.

I was very confused by this. I told him I didn't feel comfortable with that. And he said, basically, that was my own matter.

"I don't have a girlfriend so I don't see it being an issue me being with a friend," he says, raising his voice to emphasize his position.

"I am not acting like your girl, like you may be implying. I just feel like you could have shared the story of a psycho ex," I say, looking straight-ahead at the Volkswagen in front us.

We spend the next half hour on the topic, going back and forth about what is right and wrong. I guess if I had had sex with him last weekend, I would be his girl? Or I would have had more of a right to express my opinions?

Now I was thinking whether I wanted to go to Keith's house still. I felt really weird about all of this. *Why does he have to spend the night with her? Why can't he just go over early in the morning?? Doesn't she have friends of her own? Are they still having sex?* I was a little pissed off and he knew it. I think he was disappointed by my reaction since I was acting like I was his girl. Secretly, I wanted to be his girl.

We arrived at Oceania for a nice quiet, dinner. And yes, he paid, and is always generous. Now the question is, am I still going to his crib? Yes. So we drive out to Embarcadero where he lives. Before we get to his apartment, we do a little grocery shopping and get some cookies and other stuff for his fridge. I'm not the type to hold a grudge. I really like him, so my heart can soften up rather quickly when I feel like this about someone.

After settling in from unpacking the groceries, we channel surfed and got comfortable.

"Why did you give me such a hard time earlier? Isn't it obvious that I want you to be with me? I can introduce the two of you. I just made these plans weeks ago before I met you," he spoke slowly, playing in my hair as I lay between his legs.

He starts nibbling on my ear and licking the inside of the lobes. *It's starting, and I still don't know what to do.* He kisses the nape of my neck and runs his soft tongue across my shoulders. *Maybe a little kissing and playing around won't hurt. Plus, I still want to know if what Fernando said about him having a small dick is possible. But at this point, I can work with just about anything—as long as it comes with a commitment.*

He brings his hands toward me and unbuttons my blouse, while behind me. He then comes around and faces me. My hands slowly move down the back of his head, slipping down to caress his neck and shoulders. He runs his lips lightly across the top edge of my bra. I unfasten it and it falls to the floor. His breathing changes at the sight of my full breasts. He licks his fingers and traces around the edge of my nipple, slowly circling to the center. The sight of his tongue hungrily licking my nipples made me tremble. *Okay, maybe a little lick here and there won't hurt anyone.* I felt my insides do a slow, wonderful turn as my entire body registered his kiss. He takes his fingers and slowly flicks my inner lips. We're both moving with a passion of two lovers who haven't seen each other in years. *Okay, this is too much. Should I have sex? Yes or no? When was the last time he was with his ex?*

I make my way down between his legs and feel a small knob. *He was hard, but maybe not fully erect.* He slowly pulls his thumb from inside me and tastes it. He slides his tongue in my mouth and I taste, myself, getting turned on even more. He moves way down and starts kissing my waist, belly button, and nibbling on the outside of my thighs.

"Let's go to bed where we can relax and stretch out," he says, standing up and reaching for my hand.

Well, maybe we can just lie in bed.

"Okay," I say, feeling very vulnerable and confused.

We walk into his room, and I feel like I am on a wild safari. He has zebra prints everywhere—curtains, bedspread, and red pillows. Nice. But could a guy really put this room together alone? We lay in the bed and he climbs on top of me. *I won't do it. I won't have sex.* I feel the muscles in his back tense as I move underneath him. Slowly, but demanding, he kisses me again. He lowers his head down and pulls my panties down, taking his time. Giving me a chance to regress. But I am too weak. I haven't been licked in a long time. At the first touch of his tongue, my knees jerk. He takes me whole in his mouth like he promised, teasing my swollen clit, licking then sucking on it. He stops only when his tongue becomes tired. He raises up toward my face and gives me a wild kiss, with my juices all over his face and now on mine. He spreads my legs, assuming I'm ready and I stop.

I push him away gently. Regardless of what Fernando says or the size of Keith's dick, something is just not feeling right, something is telling me to slow down, fast!

"I'm not ready for all this. I still have a lot of questions about you and your ex. I just don't want to rush things."

It took a moment for the words to sink in. He looked at me with a blank stare like I'd suddenly turned into a stranger he didn't recognize.

"Okay, fine," he says calmly, standing up. He's naked and his erection is standing straight up between us. This is the first time I actually got to see it face-to-face. It was not quite short, but rather slim. Definitely, smaller than what I'd expected. But somehow it didn't matter what size he was. I just felt pretty bad about stopping midway, even going this far. But I was not ready!

"Maybe I should leave. It's late. Can I wash up in your bathroom?" He gives me a rag without a word and walks around putting his clothes on, like he was ashamed or just realized he was naked for no good reason.

Before we leave, we hug. He says he's okay, and he just wants me to want it as much as he does.

On our way home, I notice that he is speeding and cursing at other drivers; something he never does. I didn't quite put it all together until later, but he seemed frustrated about something. On my way home, we don't speak much, just me listening to his complaints about other drivers. He pulls up at my door forty-five minutes later and drives away after seeing me in.

He didn't call Sunday, the next day. He didn't call Monday. I cried that night because I knew I'd lost him. I fucked up, plain and simple. I called him Tuesday with some gibberish about how I apologized for leading him on. He said okay.

It's been six days since he's called me. I called him after he spent the weekend with his ex, and I asked him if we could see each other soon. He said he'd call me back. He never did.

A FEW MONTHS LATER

After Keith and I stopped speaking, I told myself it was my fault. How can I go to a man's house, lay naked in his bed, let him lick private places, and refuse him sex. It's like saying you can please me, but fuck you! I felt like I had really talked myself out of that man. Fernando told me that he was probably a dog. But I still can't get him off my mind. He always treated me so good and made me feel special. Maybe I messed up with second-guessing myself. Ever since then I made a promise that I will never hold back again with another man. If I am feeling something, I'll say it. And I won't go to a man's house without knowing what the hell I want to do. I still like Keith, and I feel I love him. I heard through the small, black folks grapevine here that he now has a girlfriend—a checkout girl at a local supermarket! I told Fernando and he swore up and down about being right about why Keith was single. And the fact that he is with a checkout girl adds weight to Fernando's hypothesis about successful men with small dicks needing ghetto girls to make them feel good about themselves. But whatever it is, I can't blame Keith for this one. His dick size meant little to me. No pun intended! I'm just looking for a good man, and he was one. He had a lot of things going for him—interests, money, looks, and charisma. He had liked me because he thought I was different but had ended up being like everyone else—clueless.

STORY THREE

⚇

KENYA

29

MIAMI, FL

DATING STATUS:

*Nearing 30 with the
"Can't Find a Husband"
Blues*

NO NEED TO HURRY, BUT NO TIME TO LOSE

○○ I'm twenty-nine and a half. I feel like I am approaching
○○ some pinnacle in my life. After thirty, the chances for a
black woman to find a husband decrease sharply. We have a hard
enough time just finding a boyfriend, and the older we get the
more difficult it is. The main reason why I'm single now is that I
spent most of my twenties on my back with the wrong men. One
day, I was twenty-five, enjoying life, dating different men, going
to parties, exploring my sexuality, and the next thing I look around
and I'm thirty.

I'm an investment strategist with a nice expense account, living
life pretty good, taking trips to Brazil, Australia, and the Caribbean. I have a condo on Collins Avenue in the trendy South Beach
Miami area overlooking the beach.

Where are all the men now that I've got my head together and
know what I want? When I was younger, living with my momma
and taking the bus, they were everywhere, calling me all the time.
I didn't spend too many Friday nights alone. But now that I drive
a gold Lexus (which is paid in full), own stocks, and have a successful career, the men I meet don't last more than a few weeks.
I can't tell when I had a second date or even a third with anyone
I met recently. It's almost like they are afraid of me. Perhaps they
are asking themselves what do I need them for? All I need is a
man to love, take care of me, and protect me. I can take care of
my own bills and still have money leftover for a short vacation.

My friend Nydia always reminds me, "You live in South Beach, an oasis for gay white men! No wonder you are single. You need to be where some brothers are!" By the way, she lived in D.C.—Chocolate City—before moving to Fort Lauderdale and is still single.

I just believe there is much more to it than just moving to "where the brothers are." What about the fact that maybe it's the men who have the problem, not me. All the successful black men that I know are noncommittal or chasing after some silly, dimwit girl almost ten years their junior, who doesn't know her salad fork from her dinner fork! The few who can appreciate a woman like me, well, we haven't met yet.

Now Nydia has a point with the whole South Beach not being a place for a sister to live thing. There's not much to choose from down here; most of my friends are either gay, bi, or undecided. But I just fell in love years ago with the beach that's the closest to the Caribbean I can get and the energy and diversity of Miami nightlife.

I was raised in Prince George's County, in Maryland. PG is the largest community of wealthy African Americans in the country. The average family has an annual *disposable* income of fifty thousand dollars or more. My mother is a registered nurse and my father a county judge. Though Maryland was nice, it was just a bit too country for me. I wanted to live alone, meet interesting people, and live among the rich and chic. What better place than Miami!

I enrolled in the University of Miami my freshman year and never looked back since. My relationship with my parents is an off and on thing. They've decided since I didn't go to Spellman like my mom did, I wasn't worthy of their time or money for college. I ended up getting a Merit Scholarship and worked at the local bank my four years in school.

Since I'm into spirituality, crystals, meditation, and prayer, the beach and open skies are the ideal backgrounds when I want to connect with my inner self. And of course, my absolutely wonderful, golden tan all year round isn't a bad tradeoff either! Living in Miami has led me to date outside my race a few times because of the casual mixing of all races. I've never gone as far as white men as lovers because I am just not physically attracted to them, but they make great friends. However, I've fantasized about dating and marrying a Hispanic man. Brothers will always be my main preference, but my time is running out. Dating other types of men, though it may seem like a desperate, final measure, will raise my chances of being picked. No matter what this country tries to feed us that women are in control of relationships because they have a pussy, I am a die-hard believer that it is the man who is in control because *he* asks you out, *he* calls you, and, if all goes well, *he* asks you to marry him.

I want to have babies, have a family, and leave my hectic job for good. I even have a bank account set aside to maintain my standard of living when I do leave. I have it all planned. But deep inside, I want to marry a brother. I'm in love with their smell, walk, attitude, mind, and body.

They just can't meet my needs at this point, which is a need for a husband. Most of my female friends are single, too. Crystal, Saleema, Nydia, and myself meet each other for happy hour almost every Friday after work. In South Beach there are tons of trendy, upscale bars where all the fashionistas go, but we opt for the more raw appeal. We go to Wet Willie's to analyze our frustrations over drinks like "Call a Cab" and a few shots of tequila, flirt with the male patrons, and go home alone. Their drinks, which come in all flavors and consistencies, are served in oversized cups. The routine is after Wet Willie's, we go to the Marlin Bar where most of the black people congregate after-hours.

"Well, if it ain't Ms. Dionne Warwick," teases Crystal, holding up a giant drink called Liquid Heroine, as I walk to our table on the balcony level. She always tries to make fun of my belief in psychics. The others give me their greetings in unison. I'm usually the last one to get there and the first to leave. Though I love hanging out with the girls, it's just not as fun anymore. When the drinks hit the head, it turns into a major bitching session about men.

"Well, I don't want no man," says Nydia, while popping a screwdriver Jell-O shot in her mouth. "They need just as much as I do, and I'm enough to handle. So I'd rather take care of me than anyone else." Pointing to herself, she grabs another Jell-O shot. "Mmmmm, these things are so good. They feel like balls in my mouth," she says, giggling.

"Then don't hide it, divide it," says Saleema, grabbing a handful. We all laugh as they simulate sex sounds while eating their Jell-O shots. It reminds me of one of those Herbal Essences commercials where the women scream like they're having an orgasm while washing their hair.

We all grab Jell-O shots since it's been awhile since anyone of us have seen any balls, nonetheless had them in our mouths.

"And," continues Nydia, "I'm a sex fiend. Men are like a good song. You may listen to it and sing it in your head in the beginning, but after a while, it's the same ole tune." She starts eyeing the light skin brother with the curly hair at the bar. I'm sure he would like her comment about the balls.

"You say you don't need a man, but you be with Jack every night," I point out. Jack is Nydia's dildo, who gives her a "direct hit without all the bullshit" as she calls it.

Nydia ignores our teasing and rolls her eyes. She takes a Jell-O shot and starts playing with it between her lips while she flirts with the light skin guy. I thought she said she doesn't need a man? All this bravado is coming from the drinks, but I know Nydia like the back of my hand. She is the type of woman who would look for a man in the daytime with a flashlight!

Besides, I admire Nydia for owning up to her sexuality. She's very comfortable with her body and herself. She's also aware of the power of a woman's sex appeal and makes sure no one ever forgets it. If she could only channel that sexual energy in a positive direction, instead of jumping from guy to guy, she'd make one man very happy.

"I got a question! Who would sleep with their boss if it meant getting a promotion?" Crystal asks, totally out the blue. Sometimes we do try to get deep on issues like this, but I wasn't in the mood so I decided to have fun with it.

"Me! Especially if he is fine. What's wrong with a little business and pleasure?" asks Nydia.

"I would, too. Why do you think they are so many female movie stars in Hollywood. They didn't get there because of their grand acting ability because most of them can't act for shit!" I point out.

"That's not fair," says Saleema. "So if a woman is in a high position that automatically means she slept with a man to get there?" She looks at me.

"Not all women. But there are those who do. Come on, you can't be that naive," I say to Saleema, reaching for my drink.

"I don't think I could sleep with my boss. That just would get too messy. He may want more sex. Or some other favors. Or he or I might become attached to each other. Then, on top of that, you have to work together like nothing is going on!" Saleema made a good point.

"I'd still do it," I say, sticking to my guns, "but it would have to be *my* decision. It can't be nothing like you do this or die. I'd have to really feel comfortable about it."

"It's so much easier to say that now. But when you're in the situation, things are different. Some old crusty, white man with no teeth breathing heavy, talking about how he wants you to rock his world? Please!" Crystal says, frowning and waving her hand like she was shooing a fly away.

We spend the next hour and a half talking about who bumped into their ex, why they are better than their current boyfriend's girlfriend, and how men don't understand them. All the while we're drinking our frozen daiquiris, Call-a-Cabs, Liquid Heroines, and, of course, Cosmopolitans. As the night falls, South Beach lights up: car stereos booming music and impatient drivers honking horns on jam-packed Ocean Drive. I lean over the balcony next to our table and see what all the commotion is about.

"If you're thinking about jumping, let's go to the Delano. In case we sue for faulty workmanship on that balcony, they have more money than this place." Crystal always has a scheme up her sleeve.

"If ya'll keep talking about men shit all the time, I may," I say, sitting down.

Everyone looks at me bewildered.

"I came here with ya'll to get my mind off men and that's all you can talk about," I say to no one in particular. "It's just a reminder of what I don't have—what we all are missing."

"I just like dick. That's my favorite topic," professes Nydia. Somehow we all believe that one.

I take out twenty-five dollars from my pocket and put down my half for the drinks. Feeling bad, I say, "Look, I'm not angry, just tired."

"Girl, you are putting too much pressure on yourself. Relax," Nydia says, rubbing my shoulders.

"I got some things to do at home, but call me later," I say to everyone as I leave.

"What about the Marlin Bar?" asks Saleema. At twenty-six, Saleema is the baby of the group. She looked disappointed since I go practically every week. "They're having a fashion show tonight," she says, as if that would change my mind.

"The same people will be there next Friday. I'm not missing a thing." I go around and give my girls hugs. It can be a love-hate thing at times with them. "Bye, ya'll," I say, relieved that it's over.

About 4 A.M., Nydia calls me and says everyone that night had a blast! Saleema and Crystal even met some new guys. She always has to rub things in.

I wake up just before sunrise and make up my mind to get back into jogging. Get myself looking fit again! I've been through all the self-help books, and I'm getting the inner beauty things together. But it makes me feel good to look good on the outside, too. I think about calling Nydia to see if she wants to go jogging, but I remembered she just got in a few hours ago.

After jogging for about forty-five minutes along the shore, I sit on the sand and get my head together. I missed the sunrise, but all the beauty is still there. There's nothing like the quietness of the morning when you can listen to your deepest thoughts, needs, and fears. Sitting on the sand after jogging, I begin meditating, close my eyes, and create the images in my head that I want in my life. I heard if you do this often, at least one of your images will come to be. I picture myself married in a short, white dress, my husband and I driving away in a motorcycle tagged JUST MAR-RIED. I picture myself happily pregnant and holding a small baby in a family picture. I picture a husband who looks like Terrell Davis bringing me to orgasms and neck-breaking sex every night. I picture him stroking my hair and being my protector when I need him. I dream of love, lust, companionship, passion, and suc-cess. In the middle of my thoughts, a huge, gray-black dog speeds past me and kicks sand in my face.

When I look up, I see a six foot one, thick-bodied frame walking my way. Our eyes meet as I watch him call after his dog, who is rac-ing ahead of him. He starts talking to me like he knew me all along.

"You look like a young lady I've seen at Wet Willie's, but she meditates on Cosmopolitans." He stands there smiling smugly with his hands in the pockets of his baggy sweat pants. I couldn't get my eyes off his nicely developed chest that was very apparent through his ribbed, white T.

"You look like Orlando 'El Duque' Hernandez from the New York Yankees, if he was a cop." With his sexy, tell-all eyes, and tall, broad body, I'm sure it wasn't the first time he's heard that.

He blushes. "I'm just doing my job in the area. And that means being nice to everyone, but at the same time keeping my eye on any trouble that may start. It's better than Liberty City anytime." He laughs, as his dog barks at the seagulls.

I've had my eye on this man for months! Little does he know. And meeting him like this is no coincidence. We could have met in the bar, but that would have set the vibes off all wrong. Meeting on a warm morning on the beach just after sunrise starts it off in a different way. *I wonder if he dates sisters?*

"I'm about to go wash up and get something to eat with a friend. Maybe I'll see you again at Wet Willie's," I say, hoping he'll ask for my number.

"Hopefully, I can see you soon. Maybe we can check out this café downtown."

Whoa. No beating around the bush? Just straight to the chase.

"Uhm," I hesitated, thinking fast. "I have some errands to run tomorrow." *I don't want him to think I don't have a life.* "But how's Monday night?"

"Okay, I'll call you later," he says, digging in his pants pocket for a pen.

I give him my home and work number. We give each other a

warm hug, which felt unusually familiar. I finish the jog to my condo and leave him behind.

GUSTAVO CALLS ME LATER that night. "I just want you to know, that hug felt good, like we were old friends. You have an old spirit, and you feel so familiar to me. I just want to throw that out there. Don't want to make you nervous," he says, over his barely there Spanish accent.

A man who can speak his mind and his feelings. Without trying to come off all cool like he doesn't have a care in the world. He seems like a passionate person.

"A few other people have said I have an old spirit. Honestly, at times I feel like I used to be some old village wise woman in another life," I say.

"That's cool because you seem somewhat spiritual. I caught you meditating until, of course, you were rudely interrupted." We laugh as we think back to his "charming" dog.

After a few minutes of talking basics of where we live, what we do, he asks the big question. "You ever dated a Hispanic man before?"

"No, but I am open to new things," I say, and leave it at that.

I have always been curious about Hispanic men. My cousin, Candice, married a Panamanian man. From what she says and from Hispanic friends I had while in school, Hispanic men are very committal. They take family seriously and get married at an earlier age. No wonder why they are the fastest-growing group of minorities in this country. Their birthrates are high and their family units strong.

When they zero in on that woman they want, their main focus is to seal the deal.

Gustavo is part Cuban and Argentinean. His father, who died about ten years ago of a heart attack, was heavily involved in pro-Castro politics in the fifties and sixties. His mother had been a university professor but became a stay-at-home mom and raised him and his five brothers and younger sister. They moved to Miami after his father died because his mother was too overwhelmed with memories. She cooked fresh food every night because with such a big family there were never any leftovers. Since I was an only child, being with a man who had a big family and was actually raised by both his parents was a breath of fresh air. I also knew that since Gustavo was family oriented, he'd want all he saw in his mother in a wife.

That night I burned some incense and reprogrammed my rose quartz crystals. Nydia had been here the other night and started playing with them. I certainly didn't want her negative energy or issues getting in my life. I've had these crystals for about a year. I bought them out of curiosity to see if they worked. After my last breakup, I was willing to try anything to help me move on. Rose quartz is known as the "love stone." Musa, the crystal guy I brought it from in Fort Lauderdale, said it enhances/strengthens love, forgiveness, and compassion and diminishes/lessens fear, anger, and resentment. It sounded good to me, so I bought a handful. Before going to bed, I wrapped my hair and thought about what that psychic, an old Russian woman I'd visited years ago had told me. She'd said I'd be married by twenty-four, have four kids, and have a job that helped people. She got the job part right, but in what job don't you help someone directly or indirectly? And what twenty-two year old doesn't want to hear about marriage and kids and happiness. I still want to believe what she said. But it's five years overdue.

MONDAY AT WORK, RICK the vice president, calls me into his office. Without a hint of small talk he cut to the chase. "Kenya, we need you to represent this office as a guest on CNBC." No questions about if I wanted to or would be comfortable talking to millions.

He continues, "They need you to discuss the airline sector and give their viewers some stock picks and overview of the industry's performance," he says, looking at me as if it's a done deal.

"Why me? I mean, there are tens of other analysts here," I ask, while hoping that rubbing the peridot stone I carry in my pocket at work will calm my nerves. I know I was supposed to sound confident with bells ringing, but I had to lay it down—why me?

"Honestly, you are just as qualified to do this as anyone else. But our firm has been getting a bad rap for not hiring enough women, and well, you know, minorities," he says, waving his glasses and looking a bit embarrassed.

"It will make our firm look good. And look at you. You're very attractive, bright, smart, and I'd like to get some of our minority bankers on the front lines. So, is it okay? It's good exposure. You've been here quite awhile now. What do you say?" he asks impatiently, but nice.

"Yeah, sure. But I'm rather camera shy. Am I going to be doing this every time the media wants someone?" I ask with concern.

"Dear, no," he assures me. "They just want someone from the airline sector. And that's you. But I'll be using others in the next several months from other areas. I want people to see Larrieux & Sutton as a place for young, bright people of all backgrounds, not old stogies like me," he says, with a chuckle that brightens his light brown skin. Rick is biracial, with an African mother and German father.

"You'll get media training from CNBC people, and they'll get you all ready. It's tomorrow. You need to be here at 7 A.M. They'll be doing a live shot from their New Jersey studios. Here's the phone number of the booker. She'll answer all your questions. Okay?"

"It's fine with me," I say, taking the number. "Thank God I just got my hair done," I say, smoothing it back.

"Thanks. It'll be fun," he says warmly, and he goes back to his work.

Before the end of the day, I make up a list of stocks to discuss, answers to the questions the booker sent, and some tips on how to talk to their viewers.

CONSIDERING THAT I HAVE to be at work so early in the morning, Gustavo and I have a late snack instead of a fancy dinner. This was cool because it gave us time to talk without the edginess or anxiety that can come with a first date.

Gustavo suggested a nice coffee shop downtown, where poets and artists hang out showcasing their work. He says he likes using this place as an escape from the usual pretentious scene of South Beach.

"What's this? It's pretty," Gustavo says, reaching over to touch my green, malachite, beaded bracelet.

I quickly move my wrist toward me, which kind of startles him.

"Oh, I'm sorry. It's a malachite bracelet for business success, power, and protection. I don't let anyone touch my beads because, okay, I know this sounds weird, but I program them." I look at him carefully, trying to figure out whether he thinks I'm some flake.

"I see. So you think I have negative energy?" He laughs, looking up from his cappuccino.

Look at the froth on his upper lip. Mmmm . . .

"It's just that I spend a lot of time putting my energy and needs into my crystals. No offense. Everybody has their thing, and this is mine." I shrug my shoulders, hoping we can move on to other things.

"That whole crystal thing sounds cool. I used to date a girl whose mom was really into that. Had huge crystals in her living room. Beautiful stuff."

Stuff? Crystals are one of the world's oldest resources!

"Well, I see you need some lessons on crystals and their energy." I pat his hands, while rolling my eyes. He takes hold of my hands.

"How about a lesson on Kenya and why she needs outside things like crystals?" His voice gets lower.

I laugh, mostly out of nervousness. I'd forgotten my peridot stone at home. "That's a deep question. But in this world, we can use all the help we can get," I say, reaching for my cold latte. Gustavo notices and asks the waitress for another hot mug.

Happy to change the subject, Gustavo recounts the way we met.

. . .

"IT'S FUNNY BECAUSE I live in Broward County and the only reason I came out to the beach that morning was because Papito likes running around in the sand, plus it's good exercise for him. So if it wasn't for my dog we would have never met," he says, thoughtfully taking a bite of flan.

"The only reason why I was out there so early was because it was my first day jogging in five weeks! So it sounds like there are some powers that be here," I say, dabbing my chin with a napkin. We both stay silent and bring our attention back to the poets shooting their words about love, sex, politics, and solitude.

A skinny, short, mahogany-skinned girl strolled on stage holding her head down. Dressed in a yellow-and-red wrap from her breasts to her toes, she recited a poem that spoke the words in my heart:

I saw you today crossing 23rd street
with your cornrows dancing
I thought it was you at the Post Office with a letter signed "To
Belize" by chance and
Was it you at the bar in dark jeans
sending me a smile to please?
Where are you . . .
There you go! At the museum at an exhibit alone, seeing you
taking me home
Black

I love you, but I keep missing you
I thought I saw you this morning, but I missed you
Rebirth
I hear you looking for me too, my love
Explosion in our separate paths
I'll see you when the pieces fall in our hands

A woman waiting for her love. In every guy I date, a little voice goes off inside—Can this be the one? Or is he still dealing with his drama and I with my own that our paths haven't crossed yet?

I stand up and applaud the sister. So do several other people. Gustavo did the same once he saw the response she got. The sister walked off the stage as shy but as honest as when she came on. As we get ready to go, I can't help but notice the muscles in his arms flex as he pushes his chair in and his coffee-brown skin and broad shoulders as he walks toward me to slip on my jacket.

"So are you ready for your national debut?" asks Gustavo, while we walk to the car.

"No, I wish he had picked someone else. I mean, I am ready. It's just I feel like I'm being put out to fry. I had very little time to prepare but got all my information together before the day ended," I say.

"Just do your thing. You talk to investors all the time. Most CNBC viewers are investors. Talk to them like that."

"I guess it is that easy. I'm always trying to complicate things. That's why I need *you* to calm me down," I say, rubbing the length of his arm, pleased by his useful advice.

On our drive home, I fall asleep in the car. When I get up, I worry that Gustavo would think I was being rude, but he found it soothing. During sleepy periods or right after I wake up, I tend to be the most honest because it takes awhile (and too much work) to think hard of what to really say. Suddenly, I was overcome by a feeling to be honest with Gustavo and lay my feelings on the table early—he can take it or run.

"Gustavo," I say softly, "I'm tired of playing games with men. Tired of fighting my feelings. Two years ago, I would have made you wait to even take me out and played the whole cat-and-mouse game. I like you and I want you to know it," I say, laid back in my seat. We've only been talking to each other for two days! He must think I'm crazy.

He laughs. Not quite the response I wanted. "So I'd better get you sleepy more often if this is what comes out. I've never had a woman be so honest, and yet not overwhelming, about her feelings. It goes without saying, I can easily fall in love with a woman like you," he says, and lands a kiss on my nose.

"And another thing"—he turns his body toward me—"many women I've dated would have shunned going to a coffee bar for a late evening date and would have put more value on where they were at than who they were with," he says, shaking his head.

I'M GOING TO BE on TV in an hour? *Okay . . . Northwest Airlines, Boeing, US Air . . . The sector is increasingly competitive with airlines cutting losses and increasing prices . . .*

My job sent a town car to pick me up just to make sure I got to the studio on time, and also, it was just way too early to take the train. I get to the office by 6:30 A.M. The set where I'll be sitting is already prepared. A sign reading LARRIEUX & SUTTON that wasn't there yesterday rests above the windows. A tall, skinny white girl, with cropped, brown hair, approaches me holding her makeup kit like she was Kevyn Aucoin, the famous celebrity makeup artist. Before she can even pull out her equipment, I draw out my small case of natural foundation, brown lip gloss, and mascara. Sisters with natural beauty don't need all the extra add-ons. She humbly uses my makeup instead, and in two minutes I'm done.

Sitting in the chair, with a camera in my face, I can't seem to focus. Images of Gustavo's thick body and carved arms keep dancing in front of me.

"Hi, Ms. Crowne! This is the producer from New Jersey. We'll have you on right after this commercial. Please count to five. Thanks," a perky woman with an English accent announces.

In less than one minute, I'm on the air. "We have with us now Kenya Crowne, travel and leisure analyst from the prestigious firm of Larrieux & Sutton. How are you today? I hear you have loads of information for our viewers on the airline sector." I could see the anchor, a young Asian guy, on the monitor in front of me. I just wish I could see myself.

"I'm fine, thanks, Alex. And I do have lots to discuss. Including Larrieux & Sutton turning Boeing from a buy to a strong buy . . . Its price is down by sixteen percent . . ." I say, with a bright smile and feeling surprisingly confident.

This goes on for about four minutes and thirty seconds. At the end of it all, the lights go out, the cameras leave, and I'm left in the office at 7:30 A.M. with nothing to do. I thought about calling Gustavo to see if he was watching it, but it was just too early.

Later on, when I get back to my desk from lunch, I call him over a salad. "So how was I? Don't lie!"

"You were cool. You were authoritative. You practically had me ready to call my broker to invest in one of your picks!" He laughs.

ONE MONTH AND ONE WEEK LATER

Gustavo and I are seeing each other about every other day. When he works his late shift, he stops by my house about 11 P.M. I make him a plate from the night's dinner so he can take it home with him. We haven't had sex yet. When he stops by, I let him in, give him his food, a peck, a hug, and he leaves. It's so innocent, like we are friends. And nearing thirty, my maternal side is really kicking in. I want to make sure my man is taken care of!

In the past three weeks, we've been out a few times to museums, salsa clubs, nice restaurants, and the movies. We've also spent lots of time talking and complimenting each other without wondering if one of us is being too forward. He accepts and responds to what I say like the waves do to the wind. With most men I've dated, guessing games and "getting to that level" were always coming up. There were always steps to follow, points to gain or take away, and barriers to break down. Too much damn effort. By the time you get through all that, you are already exhausted before anything even starts.

One night Gustavo says the most amazing thing. "The only way you can know if you have found the right person is if they embody all the qualities of a good friend."

I couldn't have said it better myself. One night, when he stopped by after his late shift, I decided to postpone dinner until he arrived. I planned it such that instead of him picking up his plate, we would have a late, home-cooked meal together. I told my job I'd be in late, real late.

He stops by at exactly 11:03 P.M. I had a nice bath waiting for him. I slowly take off his clothes, so he wouldn't have to do a thing. He places his holster on the table, as I unbutton his shirt, my eyes canvassing the pepperlike hairs on his chest. Slowing things down, I feel the firm bulge awakening between his legs. I don't want things to get started now and give him a towel. My bathroom is the size of a small bedroom, plenty of room to stretch out and relax. But he was taking this bath alone, this time. I close the door behind me and let him relax in the warm water and aromatic scents for about ten minutes. I come in and start scrubbing his back and soaping his body down as if I was washing away his hard day's work. Without a word, just his moans, I wash his back smooth and give him a soothing shoulder massage. When I look down, his eyes are closed. I decide to leave and check on the food.

When I walk back in, he says, caressing my legs as I stand over him in my thigh-length satin robe, "Are you going to make this cool water warm by getting in?"

Can't believe this man has energy left after a fifteen-hour shift! "They'll be time for all that later," I say softly, stroking his tight, curly hair.

He gets out of the tub and I give him one of my robes. We have fun with that. My robes are all satin with roses, or solid pinks and purple. I don't wear nightgowns. I like the idea of walking around in a robe, then just sleeping in the buff.

Dressed in a hot pink robe with red lining, Gustavo makes his way downstairs following the smell of food. We watch the late show on TV and have a quiet meal of shrimp and pasta.

After washing the dishes, we watch *The Best Man*, a tape I'd forgotten to bring back to the store. He is off tomorrow, and from the ways things are going, I may be off, too. Throughout the movie, he plays in my hair and nibbles on my ears and neck. I turn around and face him, and he gives me a full, hungry kiss. His lips just engulf mine like it was the first time he'd ever kissed me. I disrobe him, and rub his dick, throbbing against my thigh. Overcome, I make my way down and spread his legs.

I begin to lick and suck gently on his inner thighs, as he strokes my hair. I lick his length on the sides, from top to bottom, to front and back. He starts to breathe harder and I pick up the pace, and pull him deeper in my mouth with my lips. I slowly move down on his dick and rise up again, sucking hard, and twirling my tongue around it. He starts to moan now, from the incredible sensation of my mouth around his dick and the sight of me enjoying it.

I hold his balls with one hand and use the other to gently tickle his ass. He lightly holds my head, not really guiding me, but savoring the feeling. I hear him mumble something about he is about to come, but I ignore it. I just kept pumping away at him, falling in love by the second. He explodes into my mouth. I

milk him dry with my hand and swallow most of his come without thinking. I look up and see a dazed look in his eyes that told
me things were just getting started.

"I need you now, Daddy," I say, pulling him into the room. He
follows like a puppy and turns into a lion when we hit the bed.
Every few hours we wake up to do it again. He woke up nestled
between my legs in the morning. Now this is another level.

THREE MONTHS LATER

Salma, one of my clients who works in the Marketing Department
at Carnival Cruises, called me about a great, but short vacation to
the Caribbean for three nights, four days at only five hundred
dollars a person. Salma has been my client for only a few months,
but we've become rather cool, and she calls me anytime she finds
a deal. I remember Gustavo telling me that he has never been on
a cruise but wants to go on one before the year ends. I figure if
we can go away together, though it was still early, it would be a
good testing ground. By the end of the trip, we should know
whether we really can't stand each other or want to be together
for the long haul.

"Can you take off about three days next week?" I ask, calling
Gustavo from work and feeling too excited. "It's a Caribbean cruise
I want us to go on, and I need to know ASAP to get this deal I
found."

"Uhm, sure. When do we leave?" he asks, laughing. "How much
is it? I'll give you my credit card number," he says, sounding more
cooperative than I thought.

I felt like taking the card, but it was my idea, so what the hell.

"I got it! Just tell me if you are absolutely sure and I'll book it today."

"Yeah, do it. I'll give you the money tonight."

"Don't worry about it. Look, you can cover our expenses on the vacation. Okay?"

"I just feel like I gotta do something. Thank you, baby."

I call Nydia right before I leave work to go shopping with me for a few stringy things to wear. I'm more like a "whatever feels comfortable" type woman; but what she lacks in dealing with men, she makes up for in shopping for all the right things.

"I DON'T PLAN TO buy a lot because I'm going to be naked half the time," I say, smiling at Nydia as we walk down Collins Avenue on our way to a few boutiques in the area.

"All I need is a few thongs, a few bikinis, sandals, two sarongs—one short and one long."

"What about panties and something to sleep in?" Nydia asks, looking at me with her mouth open. She continues, "I hope the two of you do plan to get out of the cabin at some point! If you don't come back with a tan, everyone will know why," she says, with a look of disgust on her face.

"You can't be serious? Who's going to be sleeping? And who will be needing panties?" I look at her amused by her sudden conservativeness. "Oh no, not you trying to be Ms. Church Lady?" I joke.

"You only been with him for a few months, and you're already paying for trips," she whines. "How do you know he's not going to flip and throw your ass off the boat?" She was trying really hard to piss me off.

"Nydia, enough. It's a spontaneous, short trip. Don't hate. You know you wish you could do the same." I wish I could have taken that back as soon as it came out.

But she ignored it. She stepped in front of me, sashaying her thick hips into the Nicole Miller boutique.

Nydia is an executive secretary in a large law firm in Fort Lauderdale. Her five-foot-eight, 145-pound frame, long, wavy hair from her Brazilian mother, and caramel brown skin enable her to squash the competition in any room. But when she opens her mouth, she can spit fire. At thirty-two, she has the mind and rationale of a twenty-two year old. Dick, money, clothes are her main interests. And she takes care of all of them pretty well. I've never seen Nydia have a steady man or someone she called her boyfriend.

In forty-five minutes I am done. If I was alone, it would have taken at least two days! We stop by a takeout spot and get some wraps to eat on our way back.

"Nydia, what's up with that brother I saw you with on Lincoln Road?" I ask, trying to put the focus back on her.

"Who?" She's probably going through her internal Rolodex now. A few seconds later, she says, "Oh! That guy with the tongue ring?" She still looks confused. "Was he short?" she asks, squinting her eyes.

"No! He was tall, slim, with Cartier cuff links. . . ."

She cuts me off. "Okay, you talking about Lance." Her enthusiasm dampens. "He went to see his son in South Carolina. He'll be back soon," she says, unaffected.

I try to hold my vegetable wrap together from falling apart. I decide eating as fast as I can is the best way to prevent a mess.

In between bites, I manage to ask, "He looked like a clean-cut brother. What's up with that?"

"Lance has some baby mama drama. She's threatening to sue his ass and me since she saw us together. On what grounds, I don't know," she says, stopping at a red light. "It's too much bullshit for me. I don't need anyone else's problems."

I could tell she liked Lance, but Nydia always felt that she has to push someone away before they push her away.

We drive up to my block and before we stop at my door, I hear my phone ringing from outside. I get out of the car, thank Nydia, and before she can say bye, I run inside.

"I'm glad you're home. My mom is having a dinner tonight, and I forgot to tell you. They all want to meet you. I'll come get you in an hour?" Gustavo says, in a tone that is more like a statement than a question.

"An hour! It's a Thursday night. I just finished shopping with Nydia, I'm tired . . ."

"Come on, baby," he says, pleading. "We'll leave whenever you're ready. It's just to show our faces. I'm on my way." He hangs up.

Though I am tired, I am a bit excited about seeing his folks. His dad is a black Cuban, so his family is used to having black folks around. Also, I don't have to worry about stares—for that reason. I jump in the shower and jump right back out. I put on fitted black pants and a snug, black, sleeveless turtleneck. Sexy, but classy. I make sure I let my dark brown hair down on my shoulders so they can see that there are sisters out there with long hair of their own!

Gustavo arrives exactly one hour later. Outside, he beeps his horn impatiently. I grab my pocketbook, lock the door, and throw myself in the passenger's seat.

"Sorry, I was so rushed, but I was still at work." Gustavo leans over and gives me a big, wet peck on my forehead. I always like being kissed on the forehead because it makes me feel like a little girl. He also has this habit of playing in my hair and putting it behind my ears and taking it back out as he drives. Every man has their "thing"; I guess that was his.

"It's okay. I was just tired since I went out with Nydia to do some shopping for our trip," I say, freshening up my lipstick in the mirror.

"It's not okay because I didn't get my medicine today," he says, rubbing my thighs.

"And I know what happens when you don't get your medicine," I say, fingering his ears lightly. He likes that, too. "But this is your idea," I say, teasingly.

"I'm sure we can squeeze it in sometime," he says, with a mischievous look.

As we walk up to his parents' house in Little Havana, I get really nervous. I feel like I'm going to black out. Forget my name, what to say. Everything!

"Ay, mi hijo," says his mother, Josefina. "Y esta mujer bella?" she says, looking me up and down as we stand in the hallway. *Oh, my God, she has something bad to say already.*

"Kenya, my mom says you're beautiful." He looks at me to respond.

"Oh, *muchas gracias*. Very nice home." I kick myself inside, wondering why had I said that in Spanish. Gustavo looks at me with raised eyebrows. His mother raises her eyes, too, trying to figure me out. She leads us into the dining room.

As we walk in, there's clouds of cigar smoke, vintage Celia Cruz playing, a few couples dancing, and a few hyper three years olds running around.

Thank God it was a huge, three-story house with eight rooms. One would need a quiet place to hide from all the chaos I was witnessing.

"Gustavo," says his sister Esperanza, who stopped dancing with her little boy. "Who's the new girl?" Before he can even introduce me, all eyes were on me.

"Everyone, this is my *mujer*, Kenya. She lives in South Beach, works at an investment firm, and can actually cook," he says, laughing. Everyone follows, smiling and coming up to me and shaking my hand. I feel relieved. A woman who can cook is indispensable in a Hispanic family.

His family is close-knit, and it seems like they have been nagging Gustavo about when he is planning on settling down.

"Hijo, tienes encontrar una mujer buena y casor te ahora! A que esperas?" His grandmother would ask all the time. I think I was a solid affirmation that Gustavo was not gay or crazy.

I sit and talk to Esperanza, who is feeding her son. She's twenty-four and just got married. Her four-year-old son is from a previous relationship.

"So tell me," she inquires. "How's my brother? When are you

guys going to give me some nieces and nephews?" she asks, smiling but sincere. Without waiting for an answer, she adds, "Gustavo is always talking about you. You make him real happy, and the fact that you can cook makes my mother happy. She's been wondering where's he's been eating after work," she says, opening a can of juice for her son. "We knew someone was taking care of him once he stopped coming by for dinner," she says, a bit hyper.

"Well, it's me! I just enjoy cooking. It's really relaxing. But if we have lots of kids, then he may need to help out and start doing some of the cooking himself," I say, drinking my café. Esperanza gave me one of those "Yeah, sure" looks. Gustavo cooking? I can't picture it either.

"You're thirty. Right?" She's being a bit nosy, but I know she is just trying to look out for her older brother.

"Well, in a few months I'll be. And I know what I want, and I'm ready for it."

"No wonder you said that about having lots of kids. You want to make up for lost time!" Laughing, we both slap each other's hands because it was the truth. There was no need for me to try to explain it any other way.

I look over and see Gustavo and his brothers drinking and playing dominoes. They are drinking rojito, a popular Cuban drink made of rum, lemon, sugar and peppermint. He has many different sides to him I haven't seen. It's my first time being around his family, his culture, and the other part of his life, and I liked it.

He catches my glance and gives me a little wink. I follow Esperanza into the kitchen to help her mother. They are both talking in Spanish, then her mother turns around, strokes my hair, and starts talking in English.

"My son can be very demanding. If you two are still together, then you are doing something right," she says approvingly, handing me a platter of plantains, which was only the beginning of a dinner fit for a banquet. Esperanza and I walk out to the table and place down the platters of *arroz con pollo* (rice with chicken), *maduros* (sweet plantains), *bacalao a la cerito* (baked codfish), *pollo de la guayaba dulce* (sweet guava chicken), *boliche* (pot roast), *papas brava* (spanish potatoes), *chimichurri* (meat sauce), *frijoles negros* (black beans), *lechon asado* (roast pork) and, of course, vegetables.

I don't know when those people found time to eat their food. There was constant talking, laughing, and joking, and Gustavo was all in it.

"Kenya and I are going on a cruise next week. Where, honey?" Gustavo shoves a piece of guava chicken in his mouth. I knew he knew, but he was just trying to get me involved. My man is so smooth!

Esperanza laughs. "You don't know where you're going next week, but you know who won MVP in the NBA Championship in 1988. Just like a man!" she says, as she cleans her little boy's mouth.

"It's the eastern Caribbean. It's only for a few nights," I say, passing Gustavo the *boliche*.

"Ah, that's nice. It must have been your idea. I know my son couldn't think of that," his mother says, taking the bowl of *bacalo* to the kitchen for a refill. "He'll be happy sitting on the porch, watching the cars drive by, and calling it sightseeing." Josephina laughs and disappears behind the wooden shutters.

Gustavo managed to rub between my thighs with the tips of his fingers. He even managed to stick his fingers inside my pants and practically bring me to an orgasm at the table. I had to excuse myself and finish the job in the bathroom. A few minutes later he comes in and we have a quickie in the second-floor bathroom right over the toilet. *Oh, my Lord, this man has got me going crazy.*

We walk back to the table about several minutes later. I don't think anyone even missed us. The conversation did not even skip a beat. They were all having multiple conversations about gossip and about the latest happenings in Miami and Cuban politics. I quietly finish my plate, still thinking about the bathroom. I couldn't wait to get home. Gustavo, looked at me and gave me a look that says he was thinking the same thing, too.

IT'S THE DAY BEFORE our cruise, and we are acting like two little kids. We spent most of the day trying to find Gustavo a nice, white linen shorts outfit. The one he wanted to wear had gotten stained accidentally by his dog, so we bought a new one. We also got a few treats like chocolate body butter and erotic movies to make things more memorable. I bought some massage oils, a feathery scarf, and a see-through bodysuit he picked out. He bought a pack of socks for himself.

We spend the night trying our new little toys and oils. In the morning, we overslept but woke up in time for our car pickup to the dock. The next three days were like a dream. It was when I knew that I wanted, really wanted, this man to be my husband. We made love anywhere we could find besides the cabin and met some great people, ate fantastic food, and partied all three nights.

A FEW MONTHS LATER

Since we got back from the cruise, we have been on a natural high. Everything is going so well. We are in each other's face every day and loving it. The sex is even more explosive, more passionate. But what now? I know we are getting serious and feel any day he will pop the question. But he being Hispanic has me doubting whether he is really the one for me. What if he finds some sexy, Jennifer Lopez–salsa dancing–*mamasita* and leaves me for her? He's a good man for sure, but the question still lingers: Why can't I find a brother to love me like he does?

CANDICE CALLS ME AND says she saw James, my ex, in a restaurant with some friends—all male. My curiosity peaked. She says, James asked her all kinds of questions about me: if I still live at the same place, where I work, if I am seeing someone.

I met James my senior year at UM, but we didn't start dating until after I graduated. He was a few years older than me, ambitious and driven. When we were together, I figured out that both of our incomes would amount to nearly $175,000—after taxes. I had it all planned: where we would live, what kind of house we'd buy. We were together for two years, and he seemed ready to do the marriage thing. But he would always complain that I was "too emotional, too intense." Whereas, Gustavo describes me as "emotionally mature," "a real woman."

From what Candice knows, James is still a computer pro-grammer at a major brokerage house in New York, and travels to their Miami offices often to troubleshoot. And he is still doing good for himself. He was dressed in a sharp Armani suit, sport-ing a brand-new Rolex, and behind the wheel of a red Range Rover.

My relationship with James ended almost three years ago. I found him parked outside his job in his then Lexus giving some young girl, who looked straight out of high school, mouth-to-mouth resuscitation, but the difference was they were both con-scious.

I was never really mad at him because we were practically on our last legs at that time. But going through that has led me to Gustavo, so something good came from it though I still have feel-ings for James. Like Gustavo, James is thirty-three now, and from what it sounds like, still very single.

James claims he is too scared to call me since our last fallout, so I made it easy for him. I bet hearing from me will make him shit in his pants.

I AM SURPRISED TO realize that I have some butterflies in my stomach anticipating his voice. When he picks up, he is obviously surprised and says warmly, "God has answered my prayers."

Since we have a few friends in common, we spent about an hour catching up on who's doing what to who.

"You looked good there on CNBC. I just couldn't stop thinking 'that girl was mine,' " he says, with a smile in his voice.

"The best is yet to come," I say a bit smugly.

Eventually, he asked me if we could see each other. I agreed.

WHILE GUSTAVO IS WORKING a double shift, I meet James after work. We drive out to Coconut Grove to get a bite to eat. As I sit in the passenger side, I can't help but look over and admire his dark brown skin and thick eyebrows. I especially missed the way he tells a story as only a black man can.

We went to a small sushi bar tucked away from the main strip. "Tell me about this man you're seeing. Is it serious?" he inquires, sitting back in his chair and admiring me.

"He's cool. It's so new, I don't know what to make of it," I lie. It's been almost six months. Gustavo and I have been talking marriage. We are in deep. But I just had to see where James fit in all this. *Why was he coming back into my life now?*

James has a way of melting my heart. Though we had broken up, we had still been together sexually, and it had only been a year since our last time. He was always excellent in bed, and we managed to keep it just that without bringing up the past. I often wonder if anything more is still there between us.

"I've been thinking about relocating to Miami in the next few months," he says, searching my face for a reaction.

"What? I thought you hated the hot weather?" I say, surprised. James disliked heat so much we never vacationed in the Caribbean.

"I've been coming back and forth to Miami for a few years now. I guess my body has adjusted, as well as other parts of me."

"Like what else has adjusted?" I fall right into his script.

"I'm just more settled. It gets predictable dating several women at once. After a while, they all look and act the same. I just want some kind of stability," he says, sounding frustrated.

I did believe this. Even when we were together, I saw that he would make a good potential husband. He always remembered my birthday, first days, and our anniversary, except the last. He just had that disease a lot of men suffer from—"pussyitus." He always had to see and sample what else was out there.

Maybe James was ready now because I'd never seen him so confident, so direct, so sincere. He is attentive and seems to have found some spirituality while I've been gone.

Plus, since everything was fine between me and Gustavo, I wanted to just see what I was missing. Just in case it happened to be James.

THE HOT AND MISTY evening enveloped us as we walked out of the restaurant with his arm around me. For a minute, my mind wandered to Gustavo. Usually, on a night like this, we'd have the best sex. Watching James drive, I couldn't help but take glances at the tent shape between his legs. *Looks like some things stay the same.*

"You want to stop by the suite for a bit?" My body must have been transmitting "I want you" radar signals.

"I can't tonight, but maybe soon."

He looks embarrassed. "I don't want to interfere with what you have now. I just wanted to spend more time with you," he says, shrugging his shoulders, "and win back that fifty dollars from the last card game we played."

I give him a sarcastic smirk and pull out my Palm Pilot. "How's Thursday evening?"

"Eight P.M. We can catch a movie or something," he says.

"Yeah, or something." I put in "drinks with the girls" in my schedule, just in case Gustavo stumbles on it.

In between conversations on my way home, I think about the plans we just made. I don't know exactly what James is trying to do. I'm open to whatever happens. We have this unspoken language where we can read the other's mind. Having sex will test my feelings for him. Then we can see what it's all about after our hormones clear. There is no coincidence about James thinking of moving to Miami. It's almost like things, if they go well, can fall into place.

"HEY BABY," I SAY, walking into Gustavo sitting on the couch watching a football game. Now that he has keys, I can't tell when he's coming over. *Thank God he wasn't near the front window.*

I walk past the TV quickly so he doesn't see the guilty look on my face.

"Where you coming from with that tight skirt?" he asks, tugging at my hem before I can reach the steps. He stands up and kisses me behind my ears. Then his eyes meet mine.

"I met Candace after work. She wanted me to come with her to buy something for her mother-in-law's birthday." I caress his shoulders, but I don't think he heard what I said. *There goes that dreamy look in his eyes.*

"Baby, what about your game? I know you don't want to miss that." I say in a sweet tone, moving his hands from my breasts.

"It's just a preseason game. What I really don't want to miss is this," he says, giving me a soft kiss. His tongue runs across my neck, stopping to kiss my glossy bottom lip. The straps of my tank top come down with one pull. Hiking up my skirt, he squeezes a handful of my ass. I stand there paralyzed with anticipation, forgetting my guilt by each stroke of his tongue against mine. He picks me up then takes me to the bedroom. While he lay kisses across my neck and unbuttons my clothes, James prevails in my mind. I hold Gustavo, close my eyes, and see James. For the first time, I have an orgasm in the first two minutes. Gustavo stares at me strangely, but his stamina just increases. Moments later I'm bellowing his name—Gustavo's, that is.

A FEW DAYS LATER

I get to the office at about 6 A.M. Thursday. I'm working on a deal team for a large pharmaceutical corporation. I'm usually the first one in, while the analyst, an associate, Rick, and Sheldon, the managing director trickle in about a hour later. I look over the pitch book Rick left on my desk last night and just think of how my role has shifted from number crunching to relationship building. When I first started, I spent countless hours building models, creating "comps," and "putting together" pitch books. After a few years at the firm, Rick is trying to "expose" me to the all the duties of his job as well as Sheldon's responsibilities. Hopefully, soon making managing director won't be so far out of reach.

As each hour goes by, I get closer to seeing James. I leave work about 7 P.M. and meet James at the Grand Bay Hotel in Coconut

Grove. When we get to his room and before I can even put down my bag, we are all over each other, breathing fast and tugging on each other's clothes. I guess going to the movies is out the window. All the passion we had for each other exploded. I had missed him so much, missed his touch, his smell. I was still in love with him.

"Can't wait to take a lick of that pussy," he whispers, as he pulls me into his kitchen. Now this is the James I remember. He sat me on the island in his kitchen, and I became his banana sundae. Piece by piece I throw my clothes off. My panties landed on the refrigerator handle, my pantyhose on the counter, my skirt and blouse on the stove. I left my heels on.

James is still fully clothed, which made it even more fun because he just had me guessing what he was going to do next. Just like old times. Once a freak, always a freak.

As I lean back on the counter, he takes strawberry syrup from the cabinet above and pours it down my small B cups, and it trickles down my sides. He sucks off each drop as it drips from my nipples. Just watching his tongue eagerly lap up the sticky syrup makes my body limp. I try to take his pants off, but he refuses.

"You're for dessert, baby," he says. "Not me."

He opens my legs and takes a baby banana and slowly teases me. He takes a small bite from it, then pushes it gently between my legs and spreads it over my pussy, which is shaven clean. He begins to eat every bit of banana off from between my legs and licks every crevice. He wipes a piece of his strawberry and banana dessert and places it in my mouth. It tastes as good as homemade!

He stands me up, with my back facing him, and my elbows

resting on the counter and spreads my legs. He takes the whipped cream can to his left, bends down and begins biting my behind gently as I bounce it up and down, greedily awaiting his kisses. I then feel something cold, and mushy being sprayed down the middle. He takes his long, fast tongue and licks the whipped cream from my cheeks with fervor, spanking me when I yell too loud. Telling me to "shut up and take it," as I smile at his commands. *He remembers how I like it.* As soon as he's done, he pulls a condom out his pocket and enters me with a force that jolted my body into orgasmic spasms. He leans over and kisses me, leaving bits of whipped cream on my face. After we are done, we both fall asleep on the kitchen floor.

AFTER WE SHOWER, I check my cell phone and see several pages. James had my head spinning so fast, I'd forgotten to call Gustavo. It's 1 A.M. and calling him now would raise too many questions. I'll come up with something to tell him when I wake up in the morning.

At about 6 A.M., James wakes up disoriented and leaping around the room for his clothes. My eyes roll back, trying to think what he is up to. *I thought we would at least leave together or maybe have breakfast.*

"Baby, I got to be to work in twenty minutes. You don't mind if I put you in a cab?" James asks, out of breath.

My heart sank. Not even a reference to what just happened last night. Not even the cliché, "So how was it?" It was like nothing.

"No problem. I'll call one now," I say, pulling the covers off me and sitting up in bed. I want to get out of here as fast as I can before I say or do something I'll regret.

I get home and call Gustavo right away. "Baby, I went out with Nydia to celebrate her promotion, got a bit drunk, and ended up at her house," I say, trying to sound cheerful.

"In Coconut Grove? Nydia lives in Fort Lauderdale. You want to try that again?" he says very coolly.

I stay quiet.

"I saw you around there after work. I was riding with my partner and saw you near the Grand Bay. However," he says, "I thought you were there for some meeting for your job or something."

"Why didn't you say something if you saw me?" I ask, a bit suspicious as to whether he was following me or just happened to be on duty right near the damn hotel.

"Look! I was on duty! And get rid of that fucking tone, 'cause you have no right to even have an attitude." Somehow hearing his tone makes me relieved that he is on the phone and not next to me.

"And come to think of it, you've been a lot more sexually aggressive than usual. Like you have your own little fantasies going on in your little dingy head." He moans and asks, "So who is it? Who've you been fucking?"

I deny every bit of it. But before I could finish conjuring up a tale, Gustavo hangs up. He's hurt. I'm confused. What was I thinking? I had a perfectly good man at home, and I had to create a problem. It was almost like if something was going too good, I felt I didn't deserve it and started questioning myself.

I call James at his job. He isn't in yet. The way he sounded he was supposed to be there two hours ago. Here I go again. Straightening things out with Gustavo is my number-one priority. I leave for work not having time to fix myself up, and spend most of my day secretly wiping tears from my eyes, disguising it as an allergy. My peridot stone would be of help, but I hadn't seen it in days.

I leave a message on Gustavo's pager before I leave, convincing him to stop by the house after work.

WE SIT FOR ABOUT ten minutes, he still in his uniform, me looking a mess with stale makeup and wrinkly clothes from rushing out of the house this morning. Then I confess—about my breakup with James, me meeting him a few days ago, and the sex. He looked at me with utter disgust.

"Thank God I didn't marry you. You even look like you were out fucking. Look at your hair. You just got the shit done yesterday!" He goes on, "Damn, I sure didn't have to see you last night to know what the hell you been up to. Just looking at you gives it away." He shakes his head in disbelief.

Sitting cross-legged on the couch with my head buried in my hands, I wish I could just scream and die. He continues his berating, which I let him do just to get it all out. If it was the other way around, I probably would have killed him.

"I feel like fucking slapping the shit of you for wasting my time, our time." Then he starts laughing at me as he sits back on the couch. "Kenya," he pauses, "you are one screwed-up bitch. But you can now do all the fucking you want with whoever." He gets up and stares down on me. "I'm looking for a wife, not some trollop."

He knew that last line would sting. And it did. He starts to leave and without thinking I jump in front of him, crying and begging him not to go.

"How can you call all calm and happy after you did that?" He starts moving toward the door with me in his way. "I don't even know you who are."

"Gustavo! Please, it was just a mistake! I wasn't thinking, please!" I loudly cry, now on the floor pulling his legs.

"See if those crystals can make up for those lonely nights ahead." Before he leaves, he gives his leg one quick jerk, and I fall back against the couch. I feel like an idiot.

I call Gustavo for weeks. At the station, his house, even his mother's house. She knew we were having problems, and in her voice I can tell she wanted to help, but her son was her son. And he did not want me anymore. He told his mother to tell me to stop calling. And he changed his phone number and his patrol routes so I couldn't find him.

He did nothing wrong to me. I was stupid to see James again. It was only a fuck, the same exact thing we did the last time we saw each other. I haven't heard from James since. Candace told me she's seen him around, but he hasn't called me at all. He's still scared of me because the only place he can control me is in bed. Me being as financially strong and capable as he is a threat and, in his mind, undesirable. At least I found out that James was not made for me, though I should have listened to my inner voice. Even during our brief encounters, I always had this unsettling feeling about him. I'm sure that bit about him possibly moving to Miami was just to get me feeling like we had a chance. That comment about him wanting to settle down was also bait. Men like

James can have their cake and eat it too for a while, but eventually swarming around all that honey will get them stung by a bee.

Now two men are gone from my life.

THREE MONTHS LATER

I have been throwing myself into my work, staying until 10 P.M. and even weekends. I can see this being the bane of my existence. Since I've been overworked, my nerves are shot. Even when my office phone rings, I jump like it's unexpected. I'm rude and abrupt to clients and even my boss. But since I've brought the firm millions in assets, they put up with me. They just assume "it's that time of the month." Actually, at this point, my job is the only thing that is constant and will be there for me.

I've gained fifteen pounds from my already medium build, and my hair is thinning. I can't even keep my food down. All of my self-help, inspirational, meditation, and prayer books are all over my bedroom and living floor. I'm trying to find anything to make sense of what I feel and give me a positive outlook. I bought a new crystal, jade, which heals karma, fosters peace in myself, and grounding to get through my day. Pieces of jade adorn my office desk and my nightstand. Sometimes, I carry a small piece in my pocket; and when I feel overwhelmed with stress, I just hold it. I've also been doing lots of talking with God and praying. All these things encompassed together doesn't take away the hurt but is just a way of dealing with it without jumping off a ledge.

I loathe coming home from work to an empty house. The routine is take a shower and straight to bed. The weekends are worse. I've totally isolated myself from Nydia and the other girls, except of course for our happy hour Fridays. But most weekends, I either just sleep, read, or go for a walk. How does one go from months of spending every weekend of frolicking with your man to clipping toenails by yourself on Saturday nights?

It's like every time I think of having lost Gustavo, I lose my breath. I was in love with him but scared of my feelings. I lost someone who loved me and the chance to be a wife and mother. There's a chance that I'll meet someone again like I met Gustavo, but it's slim and uncertain. It seems like I had learned nothing from the bad experiences of my twenties. How can I move on to another phase of my life, if I can't even get this part right?

Some of Gustavo's clothes are still at my apartment unwashed. I keep them that way so I can smell his scent. Though its been months, every time the phone rings, my heart races. Every time someone with a Spanish accent calls my name, "Ken-YAH," I hear Gustavo calling me outside. I feel Gustavo was my last chance to get that family I always wanted. And now I don't know where to start again. I spent my thirtieth birthday with Nydia, Saleema, and Crystal at Wet Willie's, drinking as many "Call a Cabs" as I could to kill the pain in my chest. But not even a few drinks with the girls can make up for having my own man, in my own bed, and back in my life. I'm alone again, but I've made a promise. The next time I have a good thing, I'm going to embrace it like I would an old friend I've been missing.

STORY FOUR

°°

ALEXIS

25
ATLANTA, GA

DATING STATUS:
*Just out of a long rela-
tionship and looking to
explore her "other" side*

UNTAMED NIGHTS, EXECUTIVE DAYS

○○ I had my first boyfriend at seventeen and went to my first
○○ party at nineteen. Born in Garden Hills, Atlanta, my parents
made sure I had a tight, small circle of friends and kept me away
from Atlanta's wild side. Life has always been ordinary for me.
After graduating from Georgia State University, I went straight to
work for one of the world's largest public relations agency. The
hours are horrendous. Sometimes I am there from 8:30 A.M. to
8:30 P.M. It was so much the norm that people changed into their
slippers right after 6:30 P.M. As a senior account executive, I push
and publicize Internet companies, old and emerging. Ask me
what's the difference between a DSL line and a T1 line and I
wouldn't have a clue. But if I'm asked what is the next story the
technology editor of the *Atlanta Constitution* is looking for, it would
roll right off my tongue. My job only goes well when I get a good
"hit" or a story in a big local or national paper. Smooching, finger
crossing, ongoing follow-ups, and occasional lying is what most
days consist of. What is most annoying to me is when we get a
nice write-up on a new Internet company only to have the company disappear from the market six to eight months down the
line. It's a real headache trying to explain to reporters what happened to the "new, hot emerging" company who I'd pushed so
aggressively just a few months ago.

There are times when I'd spend a whole day on the phone with
reporters and may have left my chair about three times to do faxes.

My routine: Get a nice, big blueberry muffin from the deli downstairs, go next door to Starbucks for café latte, make calls all morning, take an hour-and-a-half lunch, make more calls, prepare client reports, and then leave. This may sound good to some, but after a few months it gets rather boring and the ten pounds I've gained working at Furlman is not cute. I make about three hundred calls a day—new ones and follow-ups and postfollow-ups—where I leave mostly voice mails. Boring!

I've been at Furlman for a year and a half. I used to work in-house for a sports TV network—WXYN. There was lots of contact with the media, and I coordinated and attended several parties and events, including one for a TV show called, "Sports Figures and Women," which attracted lots of famous athletes, models, and business executives. It was the ideal spot for a single woman to snatch a man over a cocktail discussing who's their favorite team. Unfortunately, due to "restructuring" at the network, I was fired along with twelve other people in my division. I interviewed with Furlman the following week and was hired on the spot.

Two more months and counting and I will be on to another job. My main goal is to become a publicist at an entertainment company. Anything that will get me out of the world of geeks, DSL, T1, networking, broadbands, and IPOs! Anything that will keep me awake during the day! But for now, if I can't at least get a job that will expose me to the music or TV industries, I'll at least find the right places to be.

Balance in life is everything. Sure I get a nice check every few weeks, shop, and have a nice selection of shoes. But I felt volunteering would give my life more meaning, more balance. Just a few weeks ago, I signed up to be a tutor at a local tutoring program for elementary and high-school students. Now two days a week after work, I tutor a ten year-old boy in writing. I enjoy it because it keeps me in touch with the not-so-easy lives of others. Plus, it did cross my mind when signing up that I might meet some handsome men who were interested in helping the disadvantaged. There are no cuties around, except of course Michael's older brother, who picks him up after our sessions. He's the exact duplicate of Vince Carter of the Raptors, but married. We have suggestive eye contact, but that's it. I wouldn't dare say more than "hello" and "he was great today" when referring to Michael or answering his questions about his progess. Married men are like totally out of my realm! Going there is not even tempting but downright scary. But just because he's married doesn't mean I can't admire from afar, really a far.

Long work hours coupled with volunteering leaves me drained by the end of the day. There is no time for after-work drinks or even weekend fun. Basically, Antonio, my ex, was my life, up to a few months ago. Being that he was dull and a homebody, we never had much excitement. Oftentimes, he'd be very quiet and not communicate his feelings. We were like two people who had to be together for the sake of being together. We'd been together since high school, and he was my first boyfriend and sexual partner.

One thing Antonio and I used to do often was watch porno tapes. We used to laugh at the scenes and make fun of the women making strange faces and faking their orgasms. He would always tell me how disgusting those women were to him. But in the corner of my eye, when he thought I wasn't looking, I could see his lust for them. In the back of my mind, I always envied those women for being sexually free and doing whatever the hell they wanted without a care. Obviously, by being in movies that are distributed in an open market, they don't even mind if a favorite ex or if Grandma Bea got the word about their latest public appearance. They go for self and do for self. I know they are not the best role models because there are other ways of making money, but I just admire their audacity and nerve.

After we broke up, life became more interesting. All the things I had fantasized about, talked about doing were all there begging me to explore them. Though volunteering didn't lead me into meeting a new boyfriend, it did help me meet new people from other cultures and ways of living. Amwar, the educational director of the program, spoke French, lived in Peru, and is a graduate student at Georgetown. Diana, a Muslim woman, is twenty-six, happily married with a gorgeous, devout Muslim husband, three young boys, and volunteers on the weekends. There are a few others I've come to know, but it is Amwar and Diana who I converse with and talk to about life, career, and social matters. My job is still demanding, but lately I've been leaving my slippers at home. On nights when I don't have to tutor, I usually stop at a bar before I go home. The change in routine leaves the window open for new things, new people. Basically, since Antonio was my first, I certainly didn't want him to be my last.

I've always been a little freaky. Being single is the best time to explore all aspects of myself, professionally, psychologically, and sexually. Sometimes I think I may have been a porn queen in another life. But since my mama raised me to "find a good man," I have always been afraid to show that side. And if I did, I may jeopardize a good relationship. I couldn't even have the sex I wanted to have with Antonio. If I ever told him what I really wanted, he would have left me years ago, as stuffy as he was. Now that I am single, it is still hard for me not to worry about what men think. I am always wondering what a man would think if I asked him to call me dirty names in bed or if I sucked his dick on the first date. But sometimes I would like to do just that.

MY FRIEND RENEE RECENTLY moved here from D.C. to accept a job as a teacher, a career that she loves. It's not exactly the kind of kids she wants to teach, but she makes do. She took the job as a third-grade teacher because it beat being a substitute teacher back home. And it doesn't hurt to move back to Atlanta, where the majority of her friends are. Renee works just five blocks from me at Harry Truman Public School. It's convenient for us to meet for lunch and just talk. I haven't had a friend like her in years! She is exactly what I need in my life now. She's single, funny, and loves meeting people, with streaks of conservatism in her personality. Since she's been in town, we have been hanging out after work, on the weekends, and holidays. Unlike me, Renee is looking to settle down. The remarkable thing about her is that she doesn't have that "radar" single women give off that alerts men they are on the prowl. She's cool, collected, is very comfortable with her body and herself, and always wears a smile. Approaching men is not her thing. Renee just makes it hard for them not to approach her. Her dress style is casual, never overdressy, or desperate. I like to take it over the top with sexy, revealing outfits. But Renee has a quiet charm about her that men adore.

Our goals are the same. We have pretty much what we want in life. So the only thing that really preoccupies us at twenty-five, and many other women our age, is men and finding the right one. Since we are both single bees out for some honey, we don't miss a beat of Atlanta's wild side. We go out Sundays, Mondays, Tuesdays, Wednesdays . . .

IT'S SUPER BOWL WEEKEND in Atlanta and that only means that the city will be saturated with money, fine men, and expensive cars from out of town. Though the Super Bowl is the following weekend, many people have been arriving a week in advance. All the ballers hang out during the week, unlike the little people who go out on Fridays and Saturdays. With that in mind, Renee and I decide to do a little exploring. We hit Sugar, a hot club in the heart of downtown Atlanta, where a party for one of the players of the Titans is being given.

As we get out of my green Acura TL, a group of black and Hispanic girls in long, trench coats and stilettos run inside the club. We suspect those are the dancers. There seems to be more of a party going on outside than there is inside. Renee and I pass the beeping horns, cellular phones, a small fight with a group of girls, and the long line, and step right inside. My girl, Dakota, is one of the promoters for the evening, and that means no waiting on line for me or anyone I'm with.

At about midnight, the show starts. All the men gather closer to the stage, grab a seat, or huddle in dark corners for a low profile. Renee is a bit uncomfortable watching a group of strippers perform live on stage for a roomful of horny men, but I find it fun and amusing. One of the dancers, Moondrop, is unbelievable and has the men in a trance with her light brown eyes and, of course, her outfit. My girl crawls out in a gold cat suit with the sides, ass, and breasts cut out. Her straight hair reaches her waist as she bounces to some Miami bass music. She tore off her threads, stood on her head, opened her legs, and did a move that is hard to explain in words. She then put a plastic soda bottle inside her and popped it right out! It hit a brother right across his face. He gets up and praises the dancer and casually places three hundred dollars between her butt cheeks. The men are like babes in toyland and start throwing twenties on stage. I think she may have collected about three thousand dollars for her fourteen-minute performance. I have to work much harder to get that from the job I have now! Some things in life are just not fair, but tonight was not the time to dwell on that. For the finale, Renee and I watch in awe as all the girls walk out naked into the audience with titties bouncing, and asses flapping, and give lap dances. Some men even disappeared upstairs with two or three girls in arm. This wasn't your regular crowd of everyday joes, these men were music executives, entrepreneurs, famous sports figures, and popular rappers. The average income had to be about $250,000 and some in the millions.

While the song by the Mary Jane Girls, "All Night Long" plays, Renee and I get a little philosophical.

"My God, did you see what that woman did up there? All that money? It will take months for me to earn what she did in a few minutes," Renee whines.

Adjusting my seat and trying to control my emotions, I say, "The show was good though. The girl is just trying to pay her bills. So I can't hate on her. But you attract all the wrong kind of men, have to compete with other women, and always have that "stripper" stigma with you for your life. I'd rather pass and work a little harder for mine," I say, feeling a bit preachy and hypocritical knowing that I secretly admired the dancer.

"Okay, Ms. Freak. Whatever you say. But we all wish we had the guts to do what some of these women do up there," says Renee, pointing to the dancers' pole onstage.

"Well, I want a man who is not going to be in the strip clubs spending our money on some tramp. I'd rather strip for him and keep the money home," I say, laughing.

"True indeed," says Renee. "To the good ole-fashioned way of doing things. Cheers," she says, and we hold our glasses up. We both don't know what the hell Renee is talking about, but it sounded good and we left it at that.

It's about 2 A.M., and I see Renee in the corner talking to one of the dancers and a friend. If I know Renee well enough, and from the look of their animated, but seemingly friendly conversation, she was probably grilling the girl about her performance.

I walk past them and hear, "It's not about that. It's about feeling comfortable with yourself." I don't know who said that, but whoever said it had a point.

I walk around the club and wonder if this is where my life will be five years from now when I am thirty. Most of the dancers, after looking at them for a few minutes, look to be about my age. The crowd is mostly in their thirties with plenty of single, older women with their antennas up, looking to spot their fantasy man. By the time I get to their age, I want to be at home with my family, not up in a club looking for anyone.

There I go getting serious again. Thank God, the music distracts me. Without knowing, this tall, licorice-skin brother with a jeans suit and black cap starts to dance on me, a definite thug. He was one of the few guys in there with jeans on. Not my style. Next! As I try to step away from him, he follows me and blocks my path. He stares intensely into my face with his deep, slightly slanted eyes and does not move.

I already like his directness and start to dance with him since he is one of the few available men. I check the inventory and feel his chest, arms, and flat stomach. A man's physical fitness is very important to a girl. Plus, it's a club. There's no other place to do something like that without a good excuse. Well, he's not my type from looking at how he's dressed, but there is something intriguing about him. He makes me feel sexy in a strange way. Throughout our dancing we don't say a word to each other, just touch and stare.

After a few songs, I walk away and he pulls my hand to stay with him, but I keep it moving. I walk to the bar to talk to a guy I had been dancing with earlier in the night. Lupay, is a model from Uganda, in Atlanta to shoot a video. He buys me a drink and we discuss ways he can make it as a real model.

"You need to go to New York. That is where everything is. You don't want to start off in videos and get stuck there, like many of these girls do and can't get a print job," I say, acting like I know what the heck I'm talking about.

"Yeah, I know. I want to do runway and print. These videos are so corny to me. It just pays the bills for now." He continues talking about New York and how much he wants to move there and just needs to save the right amount of money.

The conversation is getting good, until Mr. Thug approaches the bar. He stands directly behind me, making me a bit nervous because I thought he was going to rudely interrupt Lupay. Trying to understand Lupay over the loud music and his thick accent was getting frustrating anyway. Luckily, Lupay told me he had to leave because he had his video shoot in the morning and would call me later. Cool. Perfect timing.

I turn around and talk to Mike. "I like that. You giving a brother some attention," he says, standing too close to me.

Even though Lupay left on his own accord, Mike can think whatever he wants. He buys me a Kahlua, tells me he is a construction worker, was in jail, and is very much in a relationship but no kids. Somehow, learning this was a relief because he'd be more likely to be himself since he has nothing to hide. We stand real close talking, flirting, and I can't help but get turned on by his rough edges. How does he know that I still want to get to know him after he told me all that? Maybe it was my body language that gave it away.

I innocently brush my breasts against his hand as he talks about his job as a construction worker. When he gets to the part about being jailed for a few years, which inspired him to do better,

I move closer so my chest is against his. He plays it off in a cool manner, and we continue talking about entrepreneurship and money.

I TAKE A WALK down to the basement to see if I can find Renee. As soon as I reach the middle of the floor, I am surrounded by clouds of weed smoke and people making out in the corners. Someone gently grabs my hand and asks me to be in a picture with him and his friends. After a short conversation with them, the next thing I know I am in a picture with this guy and three girls. It wasn't so bad taking the picture, but it was what the picture was taken of! One of the girls was acting like she was sticking her tongue in my ear, and the other girls were holding the guy's zipper like they were about to blow him off right there.

Renee has to be upstairs since she isn't in the basement. When I turn around to leave, I see the guy pointing at the picture showing Mike.

Mike looks at me strangely and asks, "You let that girl put her tongue in your ear?"

"Look, I had no idea what she was doing. One minute I'm in the picture, and the next she has her tongue near my ear. It was nothing. She was probably just playing around," I say, a bit embarrassed, wondering what he is thinking.

"Those girls are bi. My boy, Jason, here fucks them all the time," Mike says, sounding amused at my naïveté. Jason looks at me with a "sorry, didn't know you knew him" look.

But it was then that I realized these guys are into something totally different than what I am used to.

THE NEXT DAY

It's Thursday and we have a new client coming into the office to discuss their public relations strategies. TTM, Inc. (which means To the Moon) is a mid-sized firm that specializes in web development, design, and computer networking. The meeting is at 9 A.M., which means I don't have enough time to get my muffin and coffee. I rush in the office, gather my notes, and head to the meeting I'm already late for.

"Everyone, this is who we've been waiting for," says my boss and account supervisor, Myron, a tall, white-haired, lanky man. He looks and gives me an "it's okay" wink.

I go around the table and shake everyone's hands. The director of marketing at TTM, a slightly heavy black man, practically has a smile glued to his face. I sit next to Myron and listen in.

"Alexis will be your main contact. Kelly, John, and Steven will be on the frontlines every day making sure we have your name on the desks of reporters. Everyone, including myself, will work the hardest to make TTM the standard in web development in the Southeast," Myron concludes. He gives me a nod, signaling my turn to speak.

I sit forward feeling confident since I've been through so many of these "mi casa es su casa" introductory meetings that I basically say the same thing.

"Thanks, Myron." I stand and walk around the room. I look in the direction of the marketing director and give him a little extra smile. All in four seconds. Innocent flirting helps when working with men. It lightens them up a bit, and they tend to show more patience when doing business together.

"I am very excited, as well as my colleagues, to be working on an account such as TTM. It's new. It's different. We have come up with a large variety of ideas as discussed in our initial proposal that will position you in a way that is consistent with where you want to go. We will help you identify and achieve your objectives with taste, intelligence, and creativity," I say, pausing while giving everyone eye contact.

"As Myron said, keeping you in front of the faces of reporters is very important to us. We'll be working closely with the media to include you in trend-news-and-industry-related stories." I pause, taking a sip of my water.

"Some of our services will include image development, packaging to get you into national stories, op-ed and byline articles, inclusion in trade shows, speaking engagements, and corporate sponsorships. In the coming weeks and months we will research and identify potential client groups, formulate letters, and mailings, and present you to interested prospects. We will also be researching to track trends likely to affect your industry or company."

"And we're always here to discuss and brainstorm with you," I say, concluding my four-minute speech.

This opens the floor up, and the meeting goes on for another two and a half hours. When I get back to my desk with a blazing headache, I notice my voice-mail light blinking frantically. The calls are mostly from reporters and the rest from Renee and Mike. I call Mike on his cell and leave a message letting him know that meeting after work would be great. Before I can call Renee back, she calls me to hook up for lunch.

We meet twenty minutes later and sit by the park to eat. Renee is so thoughtful. Knowing that I'd be exhausted from my two-hour meeting and not having the energy to walk around looking for food, she buys us both a sandwich combo from the deli downstairs. It's not the healthiest of meals, but it sure helped my headache.

We walk upstairs to the cafeteria in my building. "That boy called me today," I say, taking a bite of my pastrami sandwich, trying to sound annoyed.

"Don't even try it," Renee says, laughing. "Trying to act like you don't care. I know the two of you are hooking up, so give me the details of when," she says, with her mouth practically full.

"Well," I say, licking some mustard from my fingers, "since we couldn't get together last night since I had tutoring, he called again this morning to see what was up. I just called him back and left a message saying that tonight would be good to see each other.

"So? What do you think about him? What is he about?" Renee has always been nosy.

"He's an average guy just trying to make it. He's a construction worker. Definitely not my thing, but he's different than the starched, white-collar types I'm used to. So there isn't nothing much coming out of that. We'll probably just fool around." I pause and admit, "He has a girl."

Looking at Renee, I could tell she didn't like the girlfriend part. But she let it slide because we both just want to eat.

Before I let it simmer in her head any longer, I say, trying to minimize the effect, "We will probably just grab a few drinks, talk, no big deal."

We spend the rest of our lunch talking about our morning at work and our plans for the weekend.

A half hour later when I get to my desk, I get a message from Mike.

"What's up, boo. Look, tonight is cool. We can go to Cosmopolitan at about seven. It's in midtown. Hit me back," he hangs up.

That's what I like about Mike—his directness. I call him back right away and tell him I'll meet him there. Done.

The rest of the day at work seemed to last forever. Late in the afternoon, Myron stops by my office.

"Hey, just want to tell you that you were great this morning," he says, sitting down. Oh, Lord, why is he here? He could have just called? I hope I don't have to stay late!

Smiling, I say, "Thanks. I only tell people what I believe is possible." There is some silence.

"Alexis, I know the transition from entertainment to computer chips can be daunting to a young girl like yourself."

I interrupt. "Yeah, it was tough, but there's nothing better than taking on new challenges." I am a stickler for clichés.

"Well, good! I haven't told anyone yet, but I'm leaving." My heart drops. *Oh, gosh, they are going to hire someone else who will fire everybody else. I know how new people like everything new!*

"I would like you to be account supervisor. That is why I made your entrance an announcement. You can do it," he says, looking at me to confirm his confidence.

"Uhm, sure. I'm a bit caught off guard"—Myron raises his eye-brows—"but this is a happy surprise. I have been waiting for this moment! When will this all take place?" Myron regains his smile.

"Within the following month," he says, nicely but firm.

"Sounds good. Where will you be going?" I ask out of curiosity.

"Retiring. Drained out. My daughter is away at college and I figured this is the best time to be with my wife. I spent too many years behind a desk," he says, sitting back in the chair.

"Okay, well, I'm here when you want to go over details," I say, playing with a pen.

"Great, that's what I want to hear." He walks out and closes the door.

Account supervisor? The only thing I can think of is more hours. It would be about twenty thousand dollars more, but I would not have any time to use it! Images of me always playing the bridesmaid, listening to stories of my friends and their new families, while I sit behind a big desk in a starched power suit, manless with no kids to speak of, quickly dance through my mind. No! I can't have that.

I meet Mike at Cosmopolitan, a cool, trendy bar that's always packed with all kinds of young, working people. As expected, he was looking like Mr. Goodbar—brown and yummy! He looks sexy in a stretch, blue skull cap, a FUBU metallic jersey, and dark blue baggy jeans. Over drinks, he notices my distraction at times and asks, "Okay, what's wrong?"

"Oh, it's not you," I say, playing with my rum and Coke. "I may get a promotion, just thinking about how it will change things. But I'm happy about it," I say, sounding cheerful because

I didn't want to get too deep with him at all since we're not planning to connect on that level.

"Mo' money, mo' problems," he says, shaking his head, guzzling down his Red Stripe.

Though what he'd said was short, he hit it right on the head! Though I'll be paid lots more, it will bring in lots of new problems and issues. It will definitely shoot down my chances for moving on to an entertainment company since I will have little time to look for opportunities there.

As the drinks started taking an effect, I let Mike into my fantasies. From answering his questions, he found out that I would love to have a threesome, have someone watch me have sex, and wouldn't mind having two guys at the same time. I am at first uneasy talking to him about this, but Mike has a girl. I have nothing to lose. And from listening to him, he is not the faithful type nor wants to be. He is a straight-up freak himself, having sex with his girl and another girl at the same time, but he says he wants to help me fulfill some of my fantasies. And I am interested. I don't care what he thinks of me. I just see him as an escape, a brother who I can be as nasty and dirty with as I want to be without worrying if he still thinks of me as "wife material."

"SO WOULD YOU EVER go to a strip club?" he asks quizzically.

"Do you mean male or female?" I ask, feeling quite excited about what may come out of my mouth since I never really considered it. When I went to that Super Bowl party with Renee, there were strippers, but it wasn't a strip club.

"Whatever. That depends what you're into," he says, squinting his eyes. He's not much for long answers.

"I guess I'd go to both." I pause and watch his expression. I was hoping he'd jump in at any moment, but it looks like he is waiting for me to finish. So I let my guard down and continue. "I just like having fun. I wouldn't mind seeing girls dance, too. To me it's an art form and the female body is beautiful. I really believe that," I say, nodding my head.

"Okay, but now for the question of the evening. What do you want with me?" he asks.

I stay silent trying to figure out what he means.

"You are a smart, sexy, attractive woman. We both know you can snatch one of them buppie, bourgeois brothers in suits." He drinks his beer and sits back. "So what do you want with me?"

Just before I was going to tell him how wrong he was, I stopped myself. Who was I kidding? "I just want to have fun right now. I did the boyfriend thing already," I say, looking at him with suggestive eyes. "I just want someone who can make me feel free."

He laughs quietly then says, "You bourgeoisie girls are all alike."

Now I never considered myself bourgeoisie, but maybe my way of thinking can be sometimes.

"Not all of us. You'll see."

"Let's drink to seeing." He raises his bottle and I my glass.

THE NIGHT WAS WINDING down, and Mike offered to take a cab with me to where he is meeting a friend. In the cab, we get to know each other better.

He tells the driver, "Take the long way so I can tend to some business back here," as he moves closer to me.

Our tongues tickling the other, his fingers on my nipples, and my breath in his ear left me melting in his hands. He has this nasty way of kissing, where he moans and you can hear his tongue move. I was thinking about the driver, but after a few minutes, the idea of having him in the car peeking at us through the rear-view mirror turned me on.

On the ride from downtown Atlanta to my quiet block, Mike licks my nipples and rubs my pussy with his hands. He then plays with my belly button and starts rubbing my clit, but this time with the tip of his nose. The driver was probably as hard as a brick by now. The thought of the driver watching Mike between my legs drove me crazy. Mike tried to take my clothes off to have sex, but that was a no-no. Once he got the message, he stopped and we commenced with other things.

We finally arrive at my apartment. I give the driver a slight nod after seeing him smile at me. As Mike walks me to the door, he says, "Don't be afraid if after a few weeks you find your tongue in people and places you never imagined." *Whatever you say, baby.*

The first thing I do when I get in is throw myself on the bed. Sketching out in my head the many ways this night could have ended, I look over and check my machine.

"Hi, sweetie. Haven't heard from you in a few days. Hope the job is getting better. But just hang in there, you'll be running the place in no time! Call me back. Love you, baby." My mama hangs up.

I call her right back just to get it out of the way. My older sister, Jaunice, is married and living in D.C. She and my mama are exceptionally close, but throughout the years we have parted a bit since I have started thinking for myself. Jaunice and I are twelve years apart, so we are in different worlds.

"Hey, Ma. I just got your message. How are you feeling? I miss you," sounding like the "good girl" I am.

"Things are good. Jaunice may be going back to work soon since having the baby. She is such a good mother. Yesterday, when she breast-fed . . ."

Cutting her off, "Wow, that's so good. Really healthy for the baby," rolling my eyes. "Things have been good with me, too. I may get a promotion to account supervisor." I tried to sound happy.

"Wonderful! With that extra money you can buy yourself a house or something. That's great, sweetheart."

I have no plans to buy a damn house. "Thanks, I have some things to start thinking about. But I don't start until Myron leaves in about a month. I'm in training now."

"So," she pauses, "what else is new?" Here we go. "Met anyone interesting lately?"

"Well, I've been dating. Just trying to take things slow. I have some really nice guy friends, so I am enjoying myself."

"That's right. Take it slow, date, meet their parents. It's crazy out there, you have to be careful with who you meet now." She raises her voice for concern.

"Well, besides that. Renee and I have also been hanging out after work and having lunch together."

"Has she found anyone yet?"

"No, Mama. We are both very single. In time, I guess we'll find the right person." I say, getting a bit annoyed.

"I'm just concerned. Since you moved halfway across town, I don't see or hear from you much. Just like to check on things when I have you on the phone. I want you to be happy,"

"Thanks, but everything is great. Couldn't ask for more." Yeah, right!

After a few minutes, we hang up. I understand her wanting me to settle down and all that, but I need about another year to really figure out what I want. Sure it would be great to at least meet my prospective hubby now, but I still have some things to try. Still I want to get married at some point! One day, I'll figure it out.

MY RELATIONSHIP WITH MY mama has always been a strange one. I could never sit down with her and discuss dating, sex, or men. I don't mean details, but just those knowledge-sharing conversations between mother and daughter. It is only since I turned twenty-five has she been asking me about guys. She just wants to make sure I get married one day. She never asked me about Antonio or discussed safe sex or anything of that matter. It was almost as if she believed I would not notice men until I was twenty-five! She always focused on work and school when talking to me. At times, when I wanted to talk to her about the latest with Antonio, she would trivialize the matter. Making money and rising to the top was all she wanted to hear from me. How does she know I am happy as long as I am working? My world consists of so much more.

When I told her I wanted to volunteer, she asked, "Why do you want to waste your time? You might as well be a teacher and get paid for teaching." Hearing her say something so shallow and ignorant made me keep further away from her. I used to drive across town for dinner on Sundays, but now I stay home. Also, she always throws Jaunice in my face. She's married, she's pregnant, she has such a great husband. Well, if I know Jaunice well enough, she was sugarcoating things like I do. All through our lives, conversations with our mama have always been phony. When we were really hurting inside, we had to smile on the outside. My mama was the painter of this picture perfect world—she, my dad, my sister, me, our family dog, her church Sundays and neat and tidy home.

My father, on the other hand, was just not around. He was a minister. Now he's retired and does lots of speaking engagements. He spent seven days a week in the church. When he'd come home at night, I'd be asleep or too tired. The times we were together at social events, it was as a family, but at home, we were hardly in the same room together for more than five minutes.

When I was in high school, some "rumors" about my father having affairs with some local churchwomen started going around. Ms. Pearl, Ms. Sealy, Ms. Maple, and countless other names of women were being brought up as his mistresses. I had never quite understood what would keep a preacher out until 2 A.M. on weeknights, but now I do. I resented my mama for never approaching my father about this. I even lost some respect for her after that. It totally disgusted me to see her fawn over him at dinner and events and know what was really going on. And if anyone knew what was going on, it was my mama.

There was also another "rumor" that he had had a child with a woman in South Carolina in the prime of his preacher days. It's a son who now is supposed to be about my age. But in my house, we don't speak about that, too, though I've seen quite a few letters addressed from South Carolina and the same repeated number on the phone bill. It would be okay if we all talked about these issues as a family, tackled them, and moved on. But everything being kept as a secret, being swept under rugs, while we posed as the "picture-perfect family" has always left me afraid to reveal who I really am for fear that people would disown me.

A FEW DAYS LATER

Mike and I meet again for another encounter. It's a weeknight, so I can't stay out too late. This may put a damper on things, but that won't stop me. He convinces me to go to his brother's house, who is out of town. It's been only a week since we met, and I knew that if we saw each other again after that cab thing we would have sex. We meet, get some food and some videos, and go to the apartment. I have on a slinky, pink tube dress, with long, shiny, thick cornrows. As we are going up in the elevator, he can see I'm a bit tense. He teases me and pulls my tube top down and tells me I have to learn to be sexy and relax. I'm standing in the elevator with my tits hanging out and this brother is telling me to relax! He bends down and licks my nipples. I know the guard was having a good time watching the monitor. I guess it's fair to say Mike like's people watching him.

Inside the apartment, we watch TV, eat wings, and have cups of rum and Coke. I turn into the aggressor as I can't take him lying back and making me wait until he's ready. I walk up to him and stand in front of his face. Leaning back on the couch, he instructs, "Let me see that body." He pulls down my dress and leaves only my panties. He paws my body down, silently, feeling its curves. Next, he pulls my panties down and starts massaging the lips between my legs. As he licks lightly between my thighs, I cock one leg up on the couch and start moving my hips. He lays me on the couch, and by this time I am in a dreamlike state. As my eyes roll back and I part my lips, he puts his dick in my mouth. "Damn, you look good with your mouth full," he mumbles.

I start sucking on it like a fish. He was uncircumcised, which left me with a lot to play with. To hold himself from reaching an orgasm too soon, he turns me over on my knees and enters me from behind. Not anal, because I don't go there. While he slaps my ass and talks nasty to me, I make him call me the kinds of freaky names I would normally be offended by. This goes on for another thirty-five minutes of sweating, cursing, yelling, scratching, and finally a cool shower together.

On my way home, I'm too excited. I'd never slept with any man so soon. It was very much like what I saw in the movies. I felt so open now to explore my sexuality even further. Mike isn't the only guy I'm seeing at the moment, but he is the only one who I can be a real freak with. I didn't expect to get home at 4 A.M., but time had gone by quickly. At least I'd have about three hours' sleep. If I get up and feel bad, I'll probably just call in late. But one thing I must do is call Renee. Though it's late, I know she'd want to hear all this!

. . .

"ALEXIS, YOU ARE ACTING like a fool. It's one thing to go out on a date with this guy. But to have sex with him in only one week! He was in jail, he has a girlfriend, no telling where he has been or what he has!" Renee yelled into the phone.

"We used a condom. It took a lot of time to convince him to wear it, but he did. He looks healthy, and plus, I feel comfortable with him. I can do those things and still walk away from him with my head held high."

"What about what you said of finally settling down at some point. You are only getting older. You are not some free-spirited twenty-one year old anymore, and if you were I'd still scream on you." She pauses, catching her breath. "Alexis, this guy sounds dangerous, like he can screw your whole head up. That's why so many women end up by themselves when they are in their thirties because they waste their time with guys like Mike in their twenties!"

Why did I call Renee? And why did she have to be right about everything. She doesn't have a man, but she has very focused goals on how to get one. We're both twenty-five but on opposites ends of our personal journeys. Renee is not as impressionable as me. She's more headstrong, and I think that is why I envy her. The reason she doesn't have a man is by choice. The reason why I don't have one is I just can't get one.

THREE WEEKS LATER

It's Saturday and I'm home alone as usual. Renee is out on a date with some new guy she met at her gym. Curled up on my sofa, thoughts of Mike are going through my mind. I know he sexes other girls, and he even admits it. But I don't want our boat to run out of steam yet. Dialing his pager number, I wonder what his freaky ass is up to.

In about ten minutes, he returns my page.

"What's up, baby? I see you thinking about me," he says, or rather assumes arrogantly.

"Yeah, I'm just here relaxing, watching TV. What are you up to on a night like this?" I ask, fishing for a response.

He laughs. "What am I up to? Just here with some fellas at this bar having some drinks, talking to some girls."

"Met anyone interesting?" I say, with no hint of jealousy, just curiosity.

"Yeah, there's this chick here from Barbados. You know what those girls on vacation like to do. She's ready to go home with me and my man, but she's a little bit on the chunky side. I like them slim with curves—like you."

"Oh, how sweet of you," I say sarcastically. The thing with Mike is we can talk as friends, too. There are no disguises.

"So are you going to be up? I'll call you when we leave here."

"Sure, I'll talk to you later." We hang up. I'm in the mood to see him tonight, but my body is in sleep mode.

I throw my covers over me to get ready for bed. I feel a bit lonely, but, strangely, no one else seems interesting to me but Mike, including this brown-skin cutie, Malik, who dresses in Fendi suits and Armani glasses. I see him almost everyday on my way to work. He's nice and, typically, would be someone I'd date. But everything he says is predictable. We even had lunch once. He asked me, "What are some things you'd like to do?" If I had told him go to Amsterdam and work the red light district for a week, he would have started drooling like a happy baby. What he asked me wasn't a real question so he didn't get a real answer. I think I told him something about liking movies and museums. Now if he had asked me pointed questions like, "What do you WANT to do?" Then we'd be talking! If only men knew that some women like the same things they do, maybe dating wouldn't be like reading from a script.

AT 3:30 A.M., I hear a car beeping outside. I look out and it's Mike leaning out his car window motioning me to come down. Since I had only spoken to him a few hours ago, I hadn't gotten much sleep. I spent most of the time fantasizing and the other time finding a comfortable position. At 2:30, I was just beginning to doze.

I tell him to give me about ten minutes. I run into the bathroom and freshen up. I rinse my face, rinse with mouthwash, and change into a faded jeans skirt, a tank top, and slippers. As I run down the steps of my building, I see Mike getting out of his car. I go up to him and give him a big hug. There's no one around at all. The only thing you can hear at this time are the rustling of the leaves. Practically every window is dark. One would think a Saturday night would bring out some restless neighbors.

"So what is this, a booty call?" I ask, as we lean against his car, my body pressed against his. Dressed simply in jeans and a black sweater, he smells of cigarettes and smoke. However, the scent of his Cool Water cologne seeps through.

"If it was a booty call, I would have called first," he says, holding my ass as he looks into my face. "I just took the chance of coming over. Damn, a brother got to explain everything nowadays?" he asks jokingly.

I smile, not because of his comment, but because his friendly neighbor is saying hello to me. "Well, from what I can tell. You have more than just 'hello' on your mind," I whisper in his ear. I think about inviting him upstairs, but being outdoors is comfortable, as is the mood. I didn't see any reason to interrupt that. Learning how to relax is something Mike taught me.

"What do you think I have on my mind?" His voice gets deeper as he starts grinding his hips against me and starts rubbing my ass.

Without answering, I take my tongue and trace the lining of his closed lips. I play with the prickly hair of his mustache and work my way to his sideburns, gently tickling the hairs with my tongue. He unleashes his tongue and aggressively searches for mine, as we start kissing deep and slow. On cue, we start playing with each other's tongues with opened mouths. I move my hand across his flat stomach and cup the bulge between his legs.

Breathing faster, he whispers, "Suck it." At first, I couldn't make out what he'd said, but he repeated himself.

"Suck it, now." While still holding me, he unzips his pants. Then he puts his hand up my skirt and carefully puts his finger inside me from the back. I grab onto the back of his neck as his fingers massage me beneath. I look over his shoulder and swear I see someone's blinds move. Or it could have been hallucinations, considering that I was on a natural high.

I start to massage his dick and bend over and give it a kiss. All the while, we are still up against his black Bronco not caring who might see us. He gives a low moan, as if me just giving it a kiss was not enough. He then takes out a leather jacket from his car, sits on the hood, and hands it to me. I lower my body as much as I can, pull the jacket over my head and start sucking on him. Any genius could tell what I was doing, but using the jacket made it even more taboo. He manages to keep his jeans on, while I lick and suck on his dick. At first, I'm a bit hesitant, but he keeps saying, "Nobody's around, relax." As I get into it, the jacket slips off my head. My first instinct is to stop and pick it up, but I just keep going. Hearing him moaning and ooohing really made me feel in control. As I look up to see his expression, I catch the stare of a nosy old woman, wearing a housedress and stocking cap, across the street. She is so bold, she just stood at her window with a look of disgust.

"What's wrong?" Mike asks, without looking back. If he looked back too, it would have seemed like we were up to no good. The lady couldn't possibly tell what I was doing. But she might.

"Some lady staring," I say, feeling a bit naughty.

"Then give her something to look at," he orders.

I bend down, leave the jacket on the floor, and get back to work. My head is bobbing up and down so fast, plus the thought of being watched made me get really into it. Mike seemed to be getting off on it too.

After a bit, I straighten up and wipe my lips. "Can we finish this upstairs," I say to Mike.

Stroking my face, he says, "Upstairs? That's too typical." He shakes his head and points to his left. "How about that little alley right there for a quickie."

We walk two buildings down, with his arm across my shoulders holding me near him. I put his leather jacket over an empty garbage can and bend over full of anticipation. As he enters me from the back, in the wee hours of the morning, in the building where my mama's friend lives, amid our hurried movements and insatiable appetite, I feel liberated—free to be who I want at anytime.

I MEET RENEE ON my way to work Monday morning.

"You did it where?!" she squeals.

"You heard it right the first time. Mmmm . . . it was a treat, indeed," I say, with a bounce in my step.

"Over a garbage can? Outside? Didn't you feel dirty?" she inquires, as we pause in front of her school building.

"Nobody was thinking about that at the time. I was just caught up in the moment," I say, trying to get her to see it my way and get that revolted look off her face.

"Why didn't you go upstairs?"

"That's not Mike's style. He likes doing the opposite of everything. He even eats dinner for breakfast, just because."

Renee just looks on.

"I'm kidding about that one. But really, it was something that just happened. I was feeling horny that night, it was something different, and it was exciting. Plus, he never trips. Always respects me because we are working off of his standards."

"What?"

"If he was some guy who considered women who fuck in alleys hos, then he'd probably call me just that. But he likes women like that, so it's cool with him." Finally, I see the muscles in Renee's face loosen up. "And I wouldn't do this with any other guy. They wouldn't know how to act or treat me afterward."

"Why do you have bandaids on your fingers?"

"Oh, that's nothing. I got a few scrapes holding on to that hard can. I just love looking at them," I say, holding my hand up. "You should see the bites on my back, girl," I say, sounding like a teenager showing off her first hickey. Looking at those bite marks this morning on my flawless back just proved to me the wildness I was capable of, and of course it reminded me of the moment.

Renee just burst out laughing. "If I didn't know you, I'd think you were crazy. But I guess you are now one of those sadomasochist people," she says, waving her hand. "So how do you feel?" she asks holding a fake microphone to my mouth.

"I just feel relaxed. Like nothing is as bad as we imagine in life. I feel relieved, comfortable enough with myself to do what I want. Last year, this time, I would have had a real guilty conscious. I don't want to be held down by what other people expect me to do." I pause and move closer to her. "For you, it's sex in an alley, but to me, it has so much more meaning." Trying to lighten up my serious tone, I add, "I can be a ho tonight and an executive tomorrow," I say swinging my Louis Vuitton attaché.

"You are only doing Mike, so you ain't no real ho or anything," she says, rolling her eyes with a playful smile. "But give me whatever drug you are taking because you look good for someone who just got fucked in an alley," she says, and inside I know she just gets off listening to my freaky stories about Mike.

"Different strokes, for different folks," I tease, walking away.

LATER IN THE MORNING, myron calls me into his office for one of those meetings we've been having over the past few weeks about his leaving.

"Had a rough weekend?" Myron asks, looking at my hands.

"Oh, I was doing a top-to-bottom cleaning of my apartment," I say, folding my arms across my chest.

"Sure," he says, without looking at me. I swear I see a smirk across his face.

"As you know, this week is my last. You are officially account supervisor. The change in your pay will be reflected in next week's check. Have you had any time to look over the new accounts I gave to you last week?" he asks, looking serious.

I haven't even taken those notes out my bag since he gave them to me. "Yes. I've actually looked over them a few times," I say, nodding my head. "It seems self-explanatory." I hope I sound convincing.

"Alexis, I am letting you do this because I know you can," he says, leaning forward in a whispery tone.

"Yeah, sure I can. I just want to start. It's been lots of waiting and anticipation." What I really wanted to say was, "Can't you just find someone else, I hate this company and I want to work in entertainment again."

"Good. Well, congratulations." I stand up and shake his hand. I walk out of his office feeling like a big weight just landed on me. Instead of calling my mama, I call Renee.

"Hey, girl, it's official," I say, sounding depressed.

"You sound like you have just been given the death penalty," Renee says, sounding concerned.

"Well, it might as well be. Myron didn't really ask me if I wanted to do this; he just kind of gave it to me. Plus, I didn't feel like disappointing him since he's played my mentor for a while." I pause in deep thought.

"Renee, Myron does not leave the office until 9:30 P.M. and he gets in at 6:30 A.M. What do you think that means for me? And I'm new! I'll probably have to do double his hours at first just to keep track of things," I whisper into the phone.

"Okay. Do it for a few weeks. Get that money. Save some. Leave. Then look for work. Because God knows you won't have the time to sneak to interviews."

"I was thinking that. But I want to go to New York. I want to try to get something there," I say, sounding surprised at my excitement.

"New York? It's funny because I was thinking the exact same thing. A teacher friend who works there told me she can get me a job teaching older students that pays more than what I make now."

"You know what, I'm gonna start looking in the *New York Times* and sending my résumé. By next year, we'll both be in New York giving those brothers a little southern flavor."

A FEW NIGHTS LATER
"I'm on my way to a friend's house," Mike says, on the other end of the phone.

"What kind of friend?" I ask, in a sarcastic tone.

"Someone I'm fucking. She works in the contractor's office," he says shamelessly. He continues, "I'll call you when I get there."

"For what? I may be asleep," I say, wondering what he has in mind.

"I want you to talk to her. I told her about you."

A FEW HOURS LATER, the phone rings. It's Mike. He puts the phone near his mouth and I hear all the licking sounds he makes while he is between her thighs. I also hear her moans of absolute pleasure. I am throbbing and my thighs are trembling. I start rubbing myself as I listen in like a nosy neighbor. Mike comes back on the phone and tells me how he wants us to suck his dick at the same time and lick on each other's soft places. He puts her on the phone and she says how she wants to lick me and suck on my titties. All three of us are horny as hell, and I instruct her on the things Mike likes done to him.

We are all moaning, groaning, and carrying on for about thirty minutes. I hear her sucking on his dick and him slapping her on her ass as he is inside her. When I hang up the phone, I can't sleep. I wake up in the morning with bags under my eyes.

That night had my head going in many different directions just wondering how it would have been if I was there with them and not on the other line.

ONE MONTH LATER

I did finally join Mike and his lady friend for a little escapade one evening. It's not something I'd try again. Since I like being the receiver most of the time, in a threesome, everybody works. And let's just say, I like certain things done to me but not when I have to do them to someone else (especially a female). Besides that, Mike and I have grown to be really cool friends. We have occasional sex (just the two of us) but manage to have a "relationship" where we speak every few months just to say "hello." And yes, he is still with his girl. He and I don't have sex much because I can't get into all the things he does. I know myself and know what I can't do! I'm no superfreak.

JUST WHEN MY PLANS to move to New York City were getting a bit foggy, I get a call from a major museum to set up an interview. It's not the entertainment industry, but when you live in New York City you don't have to be in the industry to get to the right people because you are living among them. Renee recently became engaged to the guy she's been dating for the past five months and abruptly moved to Maryland. I'm still single.

STORY FIVE

⚇

WACEERA

23
CHICAGO, IL

DATING STATUS:
*Attached, but still out
looking for the best man*

GET IT QUICK AND A BAG OF TRICKS

○○ WAH-sheh rah. An East African Kikuyu name. My mother,
○○ Abla, which means "wild rose" in Swahili, didn't know anything about Africa and was not really into African dress or culture.
But it was 1977, and my mom told me she saw a play in Bed-
Stuy, Brooklyn, with some friends and one of the main character's
names was Waceera. A few months later I was born. She found
out that it meant a female child who moves here and there without
any special purpose. Since then, you can say I've been living up
to my name.

I did all the right things—got good grades, did not get pregnant, and graduated from college. However, I was always the "different one," always described as "special" or "interesting." It's not
until now that I realized those were actually good-meaning descriptions. My mother raised me on her own, and I am her only
child. My father died in a car crash before I was born. When I
was three months old, my mother, at twenty-seven, left New York
and moved to Chicago, where she is the owner of a small bookstore. She never married.

I never had a steady boyfriend who lasted more than a year.
In college, I traveled and studied abroad extensively—visiting
Prague, Paris, Seville, Israel, South Africa, and London. I studied
sociology with a concentration in urban societies. As an assistant
at Global Help Reunite, a national nonprofit, I travel with my boss
to South America on relief missions. Any boyfriend I have soon

gets frustrated because I am always gone for months at a time. Sometimes, I'd come back home and find my boyfriend with another woman in the passenger seat of his car or with someone else at a party. I am never in one place long enough to establish anything. But who wants to be in one place long enough? My problem is that there are so many men all over the world! Why should I think my soul mate is sitting up in some office in downtown Chicago or at the next party at Harvest in Huron, an after-work hangout? Maybe he can be sitting in a café reading a newspaper right now in Johannesburg? Partying at Les Bains in Paris? On his way to work in London? What if I am meant to just travel, experience the world, rather than settle down with Pookie from "around the way?" Anything is possible, and my appetite is never satisfied.

MY BOSS, LOURNA, AND I are preparing a grant proposal for a relief project in Peru when I noticed her shiny new ring. A three-carat diamond ring with S1 clarity. "Oh, this thing. Andre gave it to me last night after our little stroll through the park after work," she says casually, as she flipped through a binder of statistics.

"Well, that's it!? I thought you'd be flaunting that thang, letting everyone know and at least looking a little happy," I say, kind of baffled at her nonchalant attitude. "It's an engagement ring. This is some big shit! Congratulations!" I gave her a big hug to loosen her up.

Lourna looked uncomfortable at my excitement and a bit annoyed. She got up to put the binders back on her shelf and began to clear her desk.

"Waceera, I wish I could jump for joy. But it's not about that. I'm thirty-four, this is the only man who has ever proposed to me; I feel I have no choice." Her voice starts to get a bit shaky, and I'm starting to get nervous. "He's a good man, and I just want to get married. I don't have time for all that bullshit out there."

How can she wait all this time to be proposed to? "Lourna, you've never had anyone in your life you wanted to marry?"

"Sure, but I'm not just going to propose to a man. I may have let some good ones get away, but I would never feel like he wanted me if I had to propose first. It would always be a nagging thought."

Hearing all this from Lourna blew my mind. This woman was a man magnet. All over Latin America men would fawn over her ample curves, long legs, slim thighs, long, thick gorgeous black hair, and her honey-tanned skin. She could have her pick if she played her game right. She was just way too stuck on pinning down Andre, an owner of a popular, trendy Italian restaurant downtown. She spent four years with him, "laying him right and keeping my mouth shut" in her own words. It was work for her to get Andre to propose, who undoubtedly loves her. But Lourna is that type of woman who is always afraid: afraid that her man will leave, afraid that he will find someone better, afraid she will be alone, afraid to meet someone new. Because of that she never explored relationships with other men. She felt that one day they would leave her, too, and she would have to start all over again. Marrying Andre or any man is like death to her. Once you are in it, there is no coming back.

Lourna left early to meet Andre to take care of some wedding plans with the caterer. Well, at least she has a man who is involved. And she is lucky he loves her more than she loves him. It would be ideal if it was equal, but my mom always told me a man should always love you more. It's just the way men are made that makes this more practical than the other way around.

ON MY WAY HOME from the office, I decide to stop by the bookstore. There's a cute little bookstore downtown near the Sheraton simply called Black Books. Sometimes when I have big gaps between traveling, I like to buy a book and drift away into other people's worlds. As soon as I walk in, I see my friend Iman, a short man with dreads taller than he is, but always wearing a sexy smile.

"Hey girl, back again?" he says, in his Jamaican accent. He shows me the latest books and what's flying off the shelves. I stay away from those. I like undiscovered gems, books people are not reading. I notice that there are not many people around but a brother three aisles to my left in the Religions aisle. *Hmmmm . . . likes religion? Maybe he's a conscious one, trying to find out who he is. Basically means he's confused! Next . . .*

I browse the "Psychology" section to see the latest works by Naim Akbar. Every so often I find myself glancing over at the tall brother wearing a backpack, dirty Tims, faded jeans, and a worn leather jacket. He is still standing there eight minutes later not having moved an inch! He must have sensed my stares because he began to shift his feet and turned around in my direction. I quickly reached for a book but instead ended up knocking down several books on a shelf next to me. Iman comes over, gives me a smirk, and helps me pick up the books.

I look over and see that my friend has moved a bit closer to me by the Nutrition section. *He watches what he eats? A healthy man. I hope he is not a vegetarian!*

This time we make eye contact, but he gets distracted by his pager. Damn! Doesn't anything go smooth anymore? I pick up *Love Poems* by Nikki Giovanni and make sure he sees the cover. He doesn't. I walk two aisles past him and get ready to pay the cashier. I feel like he's staring. You know we women have eyes behind our backs and can tell when a man is watching our hips or the way we walk.

I take my money out and a quick look back. He is standing by the exit. *Maybe he's waiting for me to leave?* I'll just strike up a conversation about books or something: maybe religion or nutrition.

I quickly pay Iman and turn to leave. He's gone! Oh, that bum! All that I went through to get this far! The books falling, the quick glances, the beeper! Was life meant to be this hard?

I get in my car and wait a few seconds just in case he went to the grocery store across the street. Nothing. Now I am thinking really hard to myself trying to remember this guy so I can recognize him if I see him again. *Tall, light brown skin, full beard, wore a Black Dog cap from Martha's Vineyard, had an athletic, slim build, and was wearing dirty Tims.* I sit and visualize him and take a mental picture. It's filed away.

If he hadn't disappeared I would have just gone up to him. No way am I gonna listen to Lourna about approaching men. Now I won't approach a man at a club because: (a) a club is not the best

place to meet any man, (b) if he is in a club and not approaching
me after I give him the green light, that's a red flag—he may be
gay or attached. Approaching men in neutral settings like a museum, bookstore, networking event, conference, et cetera, is okay
because (a) you have the context of your surroundings to begin a
conversation with, and (b) men who go there are usually about
something more than shaking their ass and standing around in a
club holding a martini with their pinky sticking out.

Well, he's gone. He had a healthy aura, which had made him
seem friendly, approachable. And may I add if that body looked
that good clothed, I may have to hold my heart *when* I see it
unclothed. I said . . . when, not if.

I'm on my way home waiting to read *Love Poems*. Why did I
buy that book? I pull up in the driveway and park my Camry,
which my uncle sold to me early this year. Tonight, I'm supposed
to be going out with Samira, who just broke up with her man.
We usually drive around, get a bite to eat, and flirt with men at
the red light. One thing we don't do is eat and cuss about men
all night. We are not quite there yet. We are both twenty-three,
both fine, and have too many choices. Our main credo is that *we*
pick the men up, they don't pick us up.

It's about 8:45 P.M. and Samira is supposed to be stopping by
at exactly 9 P.M. That girl is always on time, too. I am fussing with
my hair, trying to get the stray strands to lie right. I can't find my
gold Wittnauer watch, so I'll have to wear my silver Anne Klein.
It's 8:54 P.M. and Samira refuses to come up to my room and wait.
My silver sling backs are no where to be found! Then the bell

rings. I grab the black mules and run downstairs. Mules, purse, keys, and lip gloss in tow, I run outside and see Samira standing by the car.

"Another minute and I was catching the bus," she says with half a smile. Samira has some bad memories of me making her wait. One night on our way to a Notorious B.I.G. concert in 1996, I was so late and unprepared, we got to the concert and were refused entry. They had given our seats to standbys. She had never forgiven me about that because it was over some dumb shit . . . I simply could not find the right outfit to wear because I'd spent the last hour on the phone with a boyfriend who wanted me to be with him that night.

"Well, your ass can go on the bus now, while I drive in my heated car if that's all right with you," I say, walking around to the driver's seat.

"Waceera, you are always so serious," Samira says, smiling. We both laugh because we know there is no way I was going to let her ride on no cold-ass, crowded bus.

SAMIRA AND I DRIVE up Freeman Avenue, while blasting music in the background, just like the brothers do. The Dragon Room, a place where they showcase unsigned acts, is packed inside, and there is a line stretching around the corner. We see packs of girls with their arms folded, in heels and short, shiny, tight dresses and skirts, shifting back and forth and every so often taking a look at the front of the line to see if it's moving or turning back to whisper about what the next chick is wearing. The guys are standing with hands in their pocket, amidst shimmers of gold, platinum, or silver chains, bracelets, and rings. Devilish eyes and grins catch our glances as we roll up, slowly surveying all the fine brothers. It's been awhile since I've spent so much time in Chicago at once, and this is what I missed the most.

"Yow! I got a Navigator, now what!?" says a gold-toothed brother standing dressed in black and gray.

"So you have jokes on my Camry?" I stop the car behind a parked minivan. "Can't a sister go out without getting any grief from tired brothers waiting on lines to get in a club?" I got a little snotty, but brothers just are not used to seeing sisters flossing, holding their own like I do.

"Waceera, he is just playing. You know how sensitive a man's ego can be. If anything, you should be saying something to those girls giving us those dirty stares." She pointed to a few girls standing outside the club with weaves so long they might trip if they walked too fast. One of them was talking really loud and all I heard were the words "cheap" and "bitch."

"I'm not paying those tired old wenches any mind. I get that every day from women," I say, turning my attention back to the brother.

"So are you just going to stand there and wait your turn? Wouldn't you like to drive around with some beautiful ladies," I say, leaning out the window and giving him my "come hither" look.

He definitely looked shocked. I bet he thought I was just going to drive away like some scared little girl. He looked at me and blushed. It was then I noticed he had on burgundy, snakeskin shoes.

"I may lose my place," he says unconvincingly. Then with his head, motions for me to come over. There is something familiar about this brother, but I can't pin it down.

I leave Samira in the car, who is already reapplying her lipstick and mascara just in case he has friends. I adjust my leather capris and turn around to grab my Fendi embroidered bag just in case I need my Mace. You never know what a stranger can be capable of doing. I step past the girls with the weaves still standing at the door and walk up to the snakeskin shoes.

As I walk up to him, with both hands in his pockets, he says, "Knocking down any more books today, miss?" Then it hit me. It's him! In snakeskin shoes?

"You look totally different! You looked so preppy earlier. There was no gold tooth!" I say, disappointed but amazed at the transformation. "Why are you here tonight?"

"They have a local jazz trio playing and some unsigned rap acts so I figured I'd come through for something different," he says, looking around. "But I see it's like a regular club scene."

Standing in front of a few guys and really close to Mr. Snakeskin, I hold my breath and say, "Why don't you come along for a ride; maybe we can hang out, play pool, get something to eat, or whatever." Looking around with raised eyebrows, I say, "I hope you have some friends."

Interested, he turns and says, "Meet my boy, Norris. He's new in town." I shake hands with Norris. Turning back to Mr. Snakeskin and extending my hand, I skipped over a very important part, "And your name must be . . ."

"Impressed." He stays silent and let's that sink in. I stare at him intensely, waiting for his name. He shakes my hand and says, "Lamont."

"Well, nice to meet you all. But my car is parked in a not so safe place. Why don't you both come and hang out with me and my girl, Samira. Use that money you have for those drinks on some real women," I say, looking around.

"Aight. Yo, come on," he says to Norris. They both walk behind me, and I could feel they are checking out my ass. Now my ass is not that big at all. It's small compared to what you see in those rap videos. But it has a small bump to it. I turn around and see from the looks in their eyes there is no disapproval. Men are so easy to please.

Jay Z's "Big Pimpin' " song starts resonating in my head. Here I am, with two fine men trailing behind me who I just picked up on a line to a club, who basically have no idea who I am, but like what they see. Guys pick up girls likes this all the time.

As we walk to the car, the whiplash in my neck I got from jet skiing in the Dominican Republic starts acting up. Norris sees me rubbing it as I take the keys out to open the car.

"You need a massage, baby?" asks Norris. "Naah," I say. "I'm alright." I notice the look in Lamont's eye that disapproved of Norris' forwardness. *Down boy. Norris will forget about me as soon as he sees Samira.*

Samira is about to catch whiplash herself if she doesn't stop looking back so hard. I give her a wink and a smile to let her know she won't disapprove mama's catch for the day.

"Samira, this is Norris and Lamont. I just saved them from "club scene hell." Samira does her leg-and-eye thing, where she seductively crosses her legs and bats her eyes at the same time. For some reason guys love this.

Lamont quietly shakes her hand. Norris moves forward and shakes Samira's hand more firmly. "Baby, those legs look good enough to eat." *Does he pull those lines out of a hat or something?* But I knew he'd like her. Norris just seems more forward and blunt than Lamont, who is more observant and cool.

We all get in the truck with nowhere to go. "So where are you lovely ladies taking us? I hope you are not planning to kidnap us and use us as sex slaves." Norris laughs. Lamont jumps in. "Maybe we can go back to my place," he suggests, looking directly at me through the rearview mirror.

"That's not exactly what we had in mind," Samira says. "Let's go play some pool and get some wings at Murray's Billiards and Grill."

Everybody was in agreement. Personally, I did just want all of us to go to Lamont's house, but I didn't want anyone to get the wrong idea. We cruise through traffic blasting Da Brat's, "What'chu Like." The song is appropriate since we are women who know what we like and waste no time in getting it.

There are some moments of silence between Samira and I talking and Lamont and Norris debating Game Six between the Knicks and the Pacers. We all start a heated conversation when Norris brings up why I approached them.

"Because I liked Lamont. I didn't see you," I said, directing it to Norris. "Guys do that all the time to us. Why should they be the only ones able to get up and pick something out that they like and take it for a spin," I say, as Samira nods in agreement but seems like she's leaving this one up to me.

"Well, I'm glad you did," says Lamont, "because honestly, I haven't been out to a club in a while, but my boy here was bored so . . ."

Norris keeps quiet for a change, letting his boy lay his game down. I turn the corner, just missing the red light, and think what Lamont is saying makes them both look good. Lamont is not the club type and Norris was bored, meaning he has no girl to keep him busy. I can see right through this one.

"Anyway, times have changed. Instead of women being pimped we doing the pimping! Keeping things in control. Making sure you brothers don't get out of hand," Samira finally says, turning around to talk to Lamont and Norris. She adjusts her skirt, and Norris keeps his eyes glued to her thighs.

"Well, that's fine with me," says Norris. "I liked being pimped," he says, laying back with his legs spread-eagled in the leather seat. "Takes a lot of work out of what a man needs to do."

"It's good to see things from a woman's perspective sometimes," I say sarcastically, as we drive into Murray's parking lot.

Norris and Samira get out first to see if they can get a good table for all of us. Lamont stays with me while I park the car in the lot.

"I got to confess," he says, opening my car door. "I saw you driving up the block and was hoping you'd stop. I was thinking maybe you was going inside the club or about to stand on the same line." He pauses. I just smiled and shook my head.

I get out of the car and walk past him without saying a word. We start walking together and I can feel the sexual chemistry seeping out of our skins! We walk up to Murray's and see Norris waving to us by a table near the bar. And from what I can see, Norris is having a good ole time with Samira, whose long legs and ample breasts always get attention. Plus, she had on a black, double-sided, split skirt and a python halter top with the front cut out, which showcased her chest even more.

Lamont joins Norris at the bar, who is getting the Cosmopolitans and Hennesseys. "Why are you giving that poor boy Lamont grief? He has been tattling behind you since you met," Samira whispers, as she sharpens her pool stick.

I thought about it and she was right. I was being hard on Lamont because I didn't want him to get the wrong idea about me. I approached him first, but I don't want him to think it gets easier after this. I still want to pose a challenge. I guess that's the difference between men and women: Men can do things and forget about it, but women just keep thinking and thinking. . . .

Lamont brought my drink and the waitress came and laid out a huge platter of chicken fingers and curly fries at our table.

Samira and I played against each other and I bust her ass. Then Norris and Lamont played. We did this for about almost two hours until it became obvious that Lamont and I were kicking some ass in the pool hall. Samira is usually good at playing, but with that short skirt on, she couldn't bend over as comfortably to get those harder to reach shots. As for me, it didn't make any difference. I could have been wearing a thong and still tried to bend over as much as necessary to win that game! I also liked teasing Lamont, who at every chance would stand behind me and give me some unneeded tips on positioning. Each time I could feel his hardness on my ass, which cost me a few shots. I just get turned on playing pool anyway. Just watching a man strike a ball in the hole drives me crazy!

During the last game between Lamont and me, I noticed some white girls just two tables down from us. I'd seen them watching when we first walked in. Actually, they had been smiling this way for the longest. Every time I looked their way one of them had on a silly smile or some curious look. I told Samira while Lamont was strategizing his shot.

"Those girls over there are tripping. They keep smiling. Is it at us or the guys?" I ask over the sharp click-clack sounds of the pool balls.

"I guess it's the guys. The one in the red camisole has been eyeing Lamont all night."

"So they want my man, huh?" I say to Samira, putting my second Cosmopolitan down.

I walk over to Lamont and pat his ass as I get ready to take my shot. "Lamont, can you help me get that green in the hole. It's way in the middle of the table."

He walks over and stands behind me, holding my arms to position me. I stick my ass out even farther and start rubbing it slowly against him. I make the shot. To thank him, I walk over to him standing against the wall and give him slow, soft kisses on the lips. He holds me closer and starts nibbling my neck. I look over his shoulder and see that white chick and silently move my lips and ask, "Want some?" She gave me one of those, "Ohmigod, I can't believe her" looks.

Can't blame the girl for being attracted to Lamont because he is one fine specimen! But I wasn't going to let anyone take him away from me either. At least, not until I'd sampled the goods for myself.

It was almost 2 A.M. and we were all stuffed and tired. No matter how much of a pool fan you are, after two or three hours of bending over you get a bit exhausted. Since I kissed Lamont, he has been attached to my hip. Norris and Samira are getting along fine just as they did from the start. Samira keeps Norris in check, which a brother needs once in a while.

I'm just amazed how everything is going so smoothly. These guys are really laid back, real cool. They paid for everything, but certainly didn't have to. And if it wasn't for that white chick trying to flirt with Lamont, who didn't notice her, I would have never known how delightful his thick lips felt in my mouth.

We drop Lamont and Norris home to find out that they both live about twenty minutes away from us. I give Lamont a hug good night, not another kiss yet. I have to keep him coming back for more. Samira practically swallows Norris whole and gives him one of those long, hot, wet ones. She comes home with me and spends the night since she lives about forty-five minutes away on the other side of town. I told Lamont to give me a call. And he will.

I throw my keys on the table and my mules on the side of the sofa. Before I can turn the lights on, I see my answering machine blinking with eleven messages. Samira gives me that look like she's about to hear some drama and all she really wants to do is sleep. She goes up to the room, undresses, and in a matter of minutes, I hear her in the shower.

I check my messages, mostly from Laurence, including several consecutive hang-ups, which I'm sure were from him as well.

Laurence's last message was, "Your ass said you would be home by 11 P.M. and it's going on 1 A.M! Call me when you get in!" His three other messages were, "Where are you?" and, "Call me back." His last one at 1:50 A.M. said he was going out. Yeah right!

I called him about 2:45 and he picked up the phone sound asleep. But he managed to get out, "Bitch, where were you?" Laurence is what you'd call "rough around the edges." He calls me his bitch, and it can mean many things—good or bad. He uses it mostly in an endearing way, but this time he was pissed.

"I was out with Samira. I'll call you tomorrow; you sound asleep," I say, in a whispery, soft tone.

"You out doing what?" he slurs.

"Baby, when you go out nobody is stressing you. I went to play pool. I'm fine, but tired. Talk to you later," I say, hanging up. That was enough for him. He'd forget all about it tomorrow.

Laurence is someone I'm seeing. We don't have titles like boyfriend and girlfriend. We've been like this for a while and it works. I know for sure he sees other women, but I am his main one. Sometimes he'll go out and won't come home until the next day. He'll says he's at "Andre's" house spending the night, as if I was born yesterday. Laurence owns three barbershops only a few miles apart. His annual income last year was in the six figures department. He owns the shop but does not cut hair. He just goes by weekly to collect his money and make sure everything is running smoothly. He also owns the four-story building that houses one of his barbershops. So he also collects rent from those twelve units—all section eight, which means the money comes directly from the city, no hassles with tenants.

Laurence, now twenty-eight, started his own business at twenty-three, after a hard time finding work after being released from jail. He was arrested at nineteen for possession and trafficking of drugs. He was part of a larger group here in Chicago but got only three years as part of a plea bargain deal. He saved the money he made from drugs and opened up his first shop. It was last year when I met him. We met at a Bulls and Knicks game. I had just come back from Spain with the most perfect tan. We met at the ice-cream stand in the stadium and have been "unofficially together" ever since. He gives me balance since my only preoccupations are my job, shopping, traveling, and men. He's not from the same background as me, but he keeps me grounded. He keeps me connected to what's really going on, since he still keeps his ears and mind in the streets. And he counts on me to give him that mental escape as I cater to his every need in food, sex, and ideas. We've also taken a few trips to Aruba and Lyon together, places he would have never been to if he was with someone else. But we have our problems, especially with him and his other women.

AT 10 A.M. SATURDAY morning, the bell rings. It's Laurence dressed in a blue sweat suit, white sneakers, black leather jacket, and platinum chain. You can never catch this man looking unkempt. He always looks like he's going out to some party or club. I quietly get up and leave Samira sleeping. I run downstairs in my cotton robe and let him in.

"Whatsup," he mutters strutting in. "I'm on my way to pick up some things for the shop. You want to come? Maybe get something to eat."

"Why didn't you call?" I asked, with sleep in my eyes. "Samira is down the hall sleeping and I have to wash up. . . ."

All of a sudden he pulls me close to him and whispers, "You think Samira would mind if we start fucking now?" I don't answer as we walk away from the front door. He starts running his fingers through my messy hair and starts smelling it. "You know I missed you last night," he says, holding me.

My pussy is starting to marinate. I start rubbing against him. I take his jacket off. He takes off my robe. He bends me back and starts licking my nipples and slides his fingers between my ass cheeks. I start moaning and rubbing his back and sticking my tongue in his ear. We walk toward the back of the couch and he bends me over and pulls my panties to the side. He takes out his "whip" and slides it in me. As I am spread and bent over the couch, he starts sliding in and out of me holding my head down. He murmurs all kinds of things to me. All I can make out are the words "sweet," "bitch," and "good." I almost bit my tongue trying to keep my moans and groans down. I love it when we sneak sex. I give it to Laurence anywhere, anytime, and anyhow he asks. My pussy is on constant call with him. And once he starts slipping in that department and giving it to other women more than me— he's out. After four minutes, we're done.

I straighten myself up and he pulls up his pants. He throws himself on the couch and stares with a smile. I knew he'd forgotten about last night. "What's for breakfast?" he asks, as he pulls me to him. Pushing my hair away from my face, he says, "By the time you get ready, breakfast at the diner will be finished. So let's make something." "We" means just myself.

Rolling my eyes, I walk to the back room and hear Samira in the bathroom. She probably heard everything and was taking her cue to leave. I walk past the door and hear heavy, fast breathing and sighing. Is she crying? I step closer and listen. Before I knock, I look through the side crack and see her sitting in the tub under the shower with her dildo between her legs. My girl must have got turned on listening to us! I start laughing quietly to myself and walk to the room. I wasn't about to disturb a sister on the verge of a climax. She was taking care of some serious business in there. I just hope Laurence doesn't have to use the bathroom soon.

A few minutes later, I get ready to use the shower and see Samira coming out. She smiles shyly and hurries past me, wrapped in a towel. "Girl, I know he's here; I'll be gone in a minute." She locks the bedroom door behind her.

Now this is the quickest shower I will ever take. One of those three-minute showers. My fine man is in the living room and my fine friend is getting ready to go out there. Samira resembles Nia Long, but about fifteen pounds heavier with longer hair. Though Laurence and Samira know each other, I always felt she was attracted to him. I trust Laurence, but he is only a man. I don't want to put him in any uncomfortable situations. I rush out of the shower and dry up in the room. I hear Samira walking to the living room. *Damn! She wastes no time. She's dressed and ready in three minutes?*

Instead of getting all dressed up, I throw on a big Donna Karan T-shirt with no panties. If me and Laurence are going to be alone, we are bound to do it again within the next hour. I take my time and walk out to see Samira standing over Laurence, who's still on the coach. Never, ever leave any of your girlfriends alone with anyone you're seeing. They may not try anything, but just the satisfaction of knowing that your man is attracted to them and they can fuck him if they wanted to is enough. I wasn't letting her have that much.

I walk past them and head to the kitchen. I hear Laurence telling her everything is going fine with the shops. Laurence is sitting watching some sports stuff on ESPN. I notice she is still out there asking him something about getting a business license. This girl has no plans to open a business. She is trying my patience. As I take some eggs out of the refrigerator, he tells her that I helped him with that and she should ask me. *Good boy.* One thing I like about Laurence is that he is very straightforward but respectful to my friends. He never engages in too much idle talk with them. Maybe because he knows, like I know. Most of my friends like him, and he feels he can fuck them anytime he wants.

Samira coolly walks into the kitchen and grabs a cup for juice. She pours herself some fruit punch and drinks it fast by the sink. "So why don't you call me tonight and let me know what you are up to," I say, looking directly at her while beating the eggs.

"Sure, I get the hint. I'll call you later." She grabs her bag. She steps back and yells bye to Laurence and leaves.

Samira just broke up with Nate, her high-school sweetheart. She's been with other guys during her "off" times with Nate because she was just curious. Now she's working as an assistant at an advertising agency in downtown Chicago. We're both just starting our careers and trying to figure out, not only what we want in life, but in a man.

I put the eggs in the pan to fry and look over and see Laurence's six-foot-three frame dozing off on the coach. When he gets up, he'll have some hot, wholesome food to eat. *These men have it so easy.*

A FEW DAYS LATER

"Why doesn't he just wait till you have children?" I ask Lourna, as we stuff envelopes during lunch for a mailing we are doing for a teacher's project in South America.

"He wants me to stop working, like as soon as we get married. He thinks I travel too much," says Lourna, sounding like she has a lot of pent-up issues.

"So tell him, you'll curb the travel, but you're not going to stop working," I say boldly.

"That's easy for you to say. I would stop working when we have kids; but now just seems like a selfish reason to me." She starts slamming down the envelopes one by one. They are not even married yet and already going through drama.

"That's one you need to straighten out. Be firm with him. Try to compromise though. Tell him you'll try to get home by 5 P.M., instead of 7:00 like you usually do."

"Maybe I will. But it's just the nerve he has to demand it that makes me mad. AggH!" she says getting up and pushing her chair in.

"Where are you going?"

"To meet Andre for lunch," she says, with a twisted smile, and walks out the door.

Listening to stories like Lourna's is one reason why marriage is a scary thought to me. Obviously Lourna is forcing herself to love this man. She'd rather be miserable with him than miserable alone. It's because of women like Lourna, who put up with shit from men like Andre that we have women in jail for killing or assaulting their partners. If something is held in long enough, it's bound to explode.

AFTER HE PICKS ME up from work, Laurence and I go back to my apartment. I see that I have several messages on my machine as usual. I haven't heard from Lamont, which means he can call anytime. Laurence's cell phone rings and he picks it up to talk to one of his workers at the shop. I use this time to take a quick run to the bathroom before I pick my messages up. I come back and hear, "Who the fuck is Lamont?" he says, waving his cell phone at me.

"What are you talking about?" Because I really had no idea how he found out.

"He's on your machine, thanking you for some night ya had." He steps too close to me. "Bitch, explain!" I hate it when he tries to intimidate me with his stance. It's like he has two sides to him.

"I was driving with Samira and she met a friend. So we all hung out. Baby, I gave him my number to be nice, that's all," I say, trying to pull his arm closer to me.

"You keep fucking with Samira, that bitch is gonna have you manless like half of these women out there. She dragging your ass everywhere when you need to be home with me," he says, with disdain, as he turns to sit down. We stay quiet for a few minutes.

He gets another call on his cell phone. He tells me one of his workers is running low on change and needs him to come through with some money. "I gotta go; we'll take care of this later." He leaves without saying another word.

I call Lamont back as if nothing had happened. No way am I getting rid of Mr. Snakeskin. He is obviously doing well for himself from the look of the neighborhood he lives in.

"Sorry I took awhile to call," Lamont says, after a few minutes on the phone. "I had a few things to do like thinking about when I will see you again."

"Anytime," I say. My aunt always told me to have a spare and pair. I have a spare and several pairs.

Unfortunately, Laurence is the type who when he doesn't like something disappears. I won't be surprised if I don't hear from *him* tonight.

IT'S BEEN TWO DAYS and I haven't heard from Laurence at all. During that time, Lamont and I see each other a few times and have dinner. He will definitely make a good replacement when Laurence is acting up. I told Lamont about Laurence, and he is okay with it. If he wasn't, he'd be out the door. Over dinner, Lamont said, "Well, I have an on-and-off-again relationship with my girlfriend. We're off now. She says she needs time to herself."

"She's probably with my man because he's had two days by himself and I haven't heard from him," I say, playing with my fettuccine. "That's good for me because that's more time I can spend with you," he says, rubbing my hand. Lamont is a trader at the Chicago Board of Trade, making him and Laurence two different men. Lamont is more pensive, watchful, while Laurence is an old-fashioned, take-charge type. If only I could wrap them up and make one.

After dinner, Lamont drops me home and goes about his business. I go home and sleep alone again tonight. At 3 A.M., I call Lamont for a booty call. He's comes by in fifteen minutes. We say little to each other because we both know what happens at this time in the morning. He walks in and we start tonguing at the door. He lifts my nightgown up and gets down on his knees and starts licking my belly button and turns me around. He runs his tongue around my ass and down between my legs. He rises and sucks on the nape of my neck. I turn around, jump up, and wrap my legs around his waist. He throws me on the same couch Laurence and I fucked on a few days ago. Just that thought drives me crazy. He takes out a condom and puts it on the coffee table near us. He lays me on my back and starts kissing my sides and massaging my nipples.

He says, "Your man know I'm stealing some pussy tonight?" I don't answer, but move my body right under his dick as the signal for him to put it in. He slips on the condom and slowly pushes his way in. Tonight I just want to get fucked, but end up frustrated. Our session lasts about three minutes with a total of one position—missionary style. He saw the dissatisfaction on my face and thought licking between my legs would help. He was wrong. Instead, he was so rough, it hurt to close my legs afterward. In these minutes of torture, Laurence was the only thing on my mind.

THE SOUND OF THE phone ringing woke me up. Since I missed the call, I get up to check for a message. It's from Laurence talking some gibberish about being sorry. This just means that he just got in from some awful sex with some new chick and feels like shit. At least, we're both in the same boat, too bad it feels like it's sinking.

When I come back to the sofa, Lamont is getting dressed. Good, I thought I'd have to tell him. Laurence has a way of dropping over early in the morning. Lamont kisses me good-bye, and we give each other quick, uncomfortable glances. I promise to call him later, which I don't.

A FEW MONTHS LATER

Samira and I meet every other weekend to go bike riding at the park near my place. We ride really slow, always getting caught up in some kind of conversation.

"You fucked Lamont? Why did you wait so long to tell me? Girl, you are crazy! What if Laurence finds out," she asks excitedly, while we trail behind several riders.

"He does his thing, and I do mine. Anyway, I'm not trying to make Lamont my man. It's something that happened. Laurence leaves me alone, so another man has to do his job. Except Lamont was underqualified."

"What do you mean? He was too small?" Samira asks, as we ride side by side.

"Now, you know I don't give details about any dick I'm getting, Samira." She looks disappointed. But a woman should never tell a friend about sex, especially how sex is with her man. Ultimately, that friend may want to sample your goods. Thinking about it again, Lamont was history, so it wouldn't hurt to indulge.

"Not only was it too thin, but he had no stamina and barely

lasted a few minutes," I say, getting flashbacks of that awful night.

Samira just looks at me with her mouth open. She can't believe it, but she says nothing.

Changing the subject, I ask, "What's up with Norris?"

"He's nice but a little too dull for me. That night when we met he was full of witty lines, but that happened to be because he was drinking a bit. When he's sober he's just about as exciting as watching grass grow." After an hour and a half of riding, we slow down to find a place to rest.

"Sometimes guys like that are cool. You are already hyper enough for two people," I say, laughing.

"I like my man to have a little spice to him, some wit, attitude, boldness. Kind of like Laurence," she says, shaking her head up and down.

"Yeah, but like any man Laurence has another side to him. He can be a handful," I say vaguely. There's no need to divulge all the fine points of my troubles with Laurence. Especially with a friend who obviously likes him a little more than she should.

"How do you take that cheating shit? I would have gone crazy by now!" says Samira.

"I don't know. Maybe that's why I cheat. It just takes the emphasis off of what he does. But I never go beyond little affairs. But you see Lamont? That's dead. The sex was not better than Laurence. So I can't waste time with that." We walk over to a sandwich bar and order two tuna subs and a salad.

"Are you going to tell Lamont it's over?"

"Over? Nothing has even started. It was just one night. When he left me that morning, we gave each other that 'see you around look.' He knows I got a man. And he has some girl he's going through issues with."

We sit in silence as we drift away in our own private thoughts. Samira has known about my little flings for a while now. And thank God, she is not a conniving backstabber. As much as she likes Laurence, I never let that threaten me. The only way she can deal with his cheating ways is with tears and fighting. That doesn't work with a man like Laurence and would just push him away farther. He's the type who needs to dig his own grave, and once he finds out the consequences of his actions, he comes running back. "Did you look into seeing if you can meet me in Chile when I go in a few months? You should get a ticket now," I urge Samira.

She usually tries to meet me abroad when I travel with my job. It's usually for a weekend or maybe more, if she uses a sick or personal day. She and I party together when all the work is done. And now that Lourna is getting married, her time will be spent calling her fiancé, waiting for a call from her fiancé, or on the phone with her fiancé.

"Yeah, my sister says she can get me a cheap ticket through her buddy pass. Lord knows, I need to get away. I haven't used any of my vacation days this year." We spend the rest of the hour eating and talking about our jobs and clothes.

Samira rides home and I ride over to Laurence's house at about noon. He reached out by calling this morning, and I figure I could do the same. As I ride up his block, I see a very dark, tall, slim, gorgeous sister walking up the street straightening her dress. She looks like she is in a rush. A rush to go where on a Sunday morning? It's definitely not church from what she is wearing. She and I have eye contact as I ride up to Laurence's steps. She was coming from his direction, but I didn't know exactly where.

I watch her disappear around the corner as I stand at Laurence's door a few minutes before knocking. I need to get myself together because my instinct is telling me that that bitch was just here. I angrily ring the bell, and he opens it within seconds, with an annoyed look. "Aww, what's up, baby?" he asks, and gives me a quick peck.

"What were you doing?" I ask, walking in and leaving the bike outside.

"I was just about to go for a jog when the bell rang. I thought it was those Jehovah people getting an early start," he says, stretching his arms and legs like he was warming up. *He did have on a running suit, so he may be telling the truth.* I guess I'll never know.

"But I guess I can go later. I'd rather do some running up in you," he says in my ear, with a deep, husky voice.

"No need to rush things. I'll be here for a while," I say, turning on the TV.

"When did you say you were going to Chile with your job because I was thinking we could take a short vacation soon," he says, taking off his sneakers.

"I'm going at the end of next month. And then we're going away again. So we can't go anywhere until fall or winter."

He stays silent. "Maybe I can meet you where you go. Come out wherever you are for the weekend or something?" *Where was all this sudden attachment coming from?*

"Yeah, that sounds cool. I was telling Samira to do the same thing." I say that on purpose to get on his nerves. Seeing that girl walking up the street has me feeling uneasy.

"Whatever, then," he shrugs and plants himself on the couch.

"How's your friend Lamont doing?" he asks out of the blue.

"I don't know. I don't talk to him like that."

"Sure, you don't," he says, playing with the remote. I am so tired of going back and forth like this. We both don't trust each other, and it's getting worse.

"He fuck you yet?" he asks, turning around and staring at me.

"NO! What is the fucking problem this morning?" I walk out of the living room into the dining room. He follows.

"Look, baby, there's no problem. I don't know. I just been feeling real weird about you lately."

"Why, because I don't be all over you and blowing up your pager like those tricks you deal with?!"

"Well, maybe! You need to pay some more fucking attention to me! Just giving up the pussy when I want it ain't enough no more. Now you starting to act like you don't want that!" he says, standing at one end of the table as I stand at the other end.

"How about me being tired of you disappearing and having sex with other people! How about that?"

This one shut him up. He'd never heard me point that out. Or ever heard me admit that I knew.

"Or how about me not knowing where this relationship stands. Am I your girl? Am I your main girl? Am I *one* of your girls? I don't fucking know!"

"Please, of course you're my girl. What kind of dumb shit is this?"

"You deal with so many other chicks on the outside, how am I supposed to know which one I am!"

"Baby, I. . . . ," he says, losing his words. I guess it's all hitting him now.

"I guess I have been a bit neglectful. Having my cake and all that," he says, throwing his hands up. "You know, those girls aren't as important as you are." He sits down next to me.

"Look, whatever. I've been out riding and I'm just tired this morning. Let's just forget this," I say, walking to the kitchen.

"No, we got to deal with this shit here. It just fucks with me that my girl think she's not my girl. That's some real bullshit," he says, looking baffled.

I leave him alone in the dining room. I look through the shutters and see him still sitting there a half hour later. For a minute, I feel bad for him because at this point, he must be feeling really lonely. Thinking all along that everything was fine and that I was happy. But knowing now that I felt like I wasn't his seems like we weren't together all along. And it's true. I didn't feel like I was his woman. But to be honest, saying that I didn't know what I was to him, protects me. If it ever were to get out that I cheated on him several times, he'd leave me for good. At least I can use that excuse of me not knowing where we stand or feeling lonely if the question comes up again. I just feel like I am probably his main girl, and that just doesn't meet my standards for a real relationship. But it still doesn't change the fact that I am *practically* in love with Laurence.

Some time passes by as we both stay in separate parts of the house. I called in two orders of some steamed fish and shrimps from the Crab Inn down the street. We've been "together" for so long, it's like everything I do is in pairs. He doesn't know that I ordered some food for him, but I know he must be hungry.

When the delivery guy rings the bell, he comes downstairs. "Thanks," he says humbly, and walks over to the couch holding the food. I go in the kitchen and get us some drinks.

We sit in front of the couch and silently eat and laugh at the TV. Laurence has one of those long, L-shaped couches so we have more than enough space from each other. The whole room just feels brightened though, like we are just starting to see each other for the first time in a different light now that everything is out in the open.

"Come here," he quietly demands. I walk over to his side and nestle my body against his in the chair. He starts rubbing my arms and shoulders soothingly. I love it when he does this. We watch MTV's *Real World* and make fun of how everybody just seems so *unreal* and overdramatic.

Laurence reaches for the remote and turns down the TV. He sits up and so do I. *Uh-oh, he's about to make a speech about something.* He starts twirling the remote in his hand, which means he's nervous. The remote drops on the floor.

"Okay, baby, what's up?" I ask, sitting up and sounding serious.

"I know I was out of sight for a few days," he says, and just when I was about to jump in, he continues. "I did some thinking after our little fallout earlier. . . ." *Oh, no, he's breaking up with me! Why? He got somebody pregnant?*

"And I want us to get married," he says, and reaches for my hand. *My heart drops. No, not that! Not yet! He loves me that much?*

I'm happy and confused at the same time. I give him a long hug and say nothing.

He looks at me and says, "I'm just tired of all these silly games. You have always been there for me. When I need time to straighten my head out, you give it to me. You let me make my own mistakes. You take care of me and yourself. You travel and are constantly learning new things. I need you," he says, keeping his voice steady, "and I love you."

I never saw this in Laurence. This is the other side I was talking about. I could marry him but not now. This certainly makes me know that I definitely underestimated how he felt about me. I guess just because a man has other women doesn't mean he wants them. Men are good at separating love from sex. But cheating is not a level I want to succumb to again.

My heart is beating faster with the good news, but my head hurts. I'm too young to get married, there's too much to do. I like having various male friends and experiencing new things. Being Laurence's wife means cooking and cleaning every single day. It means wondering if he's out cheating. He's too high maintenance. And too jealous.

"Baby," I say softly, stroking his bearded chin. "I love you, too. I just can't marry you now. I'm not ready. There are some things I still need to figure out about you. Just because I don't complain and fuss all the time about your other women, doesn't mean it doesn't hurt."

He stays silent and sits back against the couch knowing I'm right.

"It's okay. I'm not going anywhere. I want what you want, but we need to be more stable. When things go wrong, you can't just disappear. When I have male friends, you can't jump to conclusions. We have to build up to that. We can't skip that and get married." Boy, I am good!

"Okay, but at least you know where I stand." He gets up and walks outside to the garage. I look through the window and see him cleaning up some things in there.

As I wash a few of his dishes in the sink, I think about what he said. Though I do cook and clean for him, I actually enjoy it because it's by choice. I just feel that I still have some oats to sow at twenty-three. In a few months, I'll be gone for a month. Lourna and I are going as part of an entourage to Chile and Colombia to oversee a teaching program for young people. Then we are spending a few days in London to attend an awards conference for the National Association for Teaching Entrepreneurship. I will meet countless of professional men on these trips, and who knows what may become of that. It's been a few months since I've traveled like that, and I just enjoy meeting new kinds of people. Being married to Laurence would mean giving that up.

While packing away dishes, scenes from my little escapades abroad flash through my mind. What if Laurence knew? When I was nineteen, while snorkeling off the coast of Curaçao, my guide, a fifty-five-year-old man, brought me to my first orgasm. When on the boat-sailing back, as I was sitting in my bikini and feeling quite daring, he began licking between my legs until he climbed on top and I let him huff and puff until he came. Or how about in Nice, while spending a semester abroad, I sneaked a French man I had met earlier in the day at a café, into the chateau owned by my university and had rough sex with him while everyone was asleep. What would Laurence think about all that? Would he still feel the same? And I can't honestly say I will not have another rendezvous when traveling again either. Being a wanderer, it's hard to just settle in one place. It's even harder to settle for one person.

EPILOGUE

∷

ONE YEAR LATER...

FARAH, 25

CITY: Brooklyn, NY

DATING STATUS: Single (still!)

It took me awhile to get my head together after all that Marcus stuff. I was totally out of my realm dating him. It just wasn't me to date someone who's already attached. But after that ended, I just kept meeting guys who had girlfriends. It got to a point where I was like "whatever." The more often I found myself in these "situations," the sex would just get worse. However, it took one last time for me to finally realize I was going the wrong way. I was having sex with a guy, and the condom broke. He was known to be promiscuous, and I was afraid I might have caught AIDS or become pregnant. He had had gonorrhea in the past, so anything was possible. That fear sent a shock through my body, and I've never been the same since. My tests came back fine, but psychologically I was messed up.

My girl, Lola, and I still hang out sometimes, but she found herself a man. Where did she meet him? At a club! Lola is now with Marcus' friend, Steve, with the long dreads. Since they didn't exchange numbers, fate brought them together in Baltimore.

Honestly, Lola is significantly different from myself and other sisters I know. She was born in Panama, a dark-skinned sister who comes from comfortable means. She never understood how American black women were so hung up on making sure their man have all these material items, the best job, be good looking, and be the best in bed—all at the same time! It was like a joke to her. She used to slip in and out of Spanish and say, "All you *mujeres* here are living in a fantasy world." I'm beginning to understand what that means.

As "the other woman," Lola always thought I had "issues." A major misconception about "the other woman" is that she is very insecure, lonely, and has self-image problems. Actually, having sex with men who had girlfriends made me feel powerful, sexy, self-confident. It also allowed me to have some control over my feelings because I knew what the relationship would be about from the beginning. But there will always come a time when a woman will want more with that cheating guy. There is a small part that hopes he'll realize you are the one for him. Nonetheless, it's the excitement, the sex, the dining, the no-baggage or drama that keeps "the other woman" going. Though it can be exciting in the beginning, you still go home alone. You still have no one to share holidays or birthdays with.

Seeing the other side of things made me aware of the reality that men will cheat. No amount of crying or fighting will stop a man from cheating before his time. From what I've gathered, men will stop cheating when they damn well feel good and ready.

And Marcus did. He called me a few weeks ago just to say "hello." I never held a grudge against Marcus because it was me who had willingly agreed to be "the other woman." When he called, we had a light conversation, and I managed to ask him was he still a dog. He sheepishly said, "No." Marcus told me he is a faithful father and boyfriend; he said he just got tired of chasing women. He was exhausted with the back and forth and coming up with new excuses to tell his girlfriend. Marcus was one of the doggiest, nastiest, devilish, cheating men that I've met while out on the dating scene, and I used to wonder if he had a conscience.

Now, will I tolerate my man (if I get one) cheating? Yes, I would. I won't give him the green light, but I'd rather let him get it all out now before we walk down the aisle. Ironically, admitting that I can tolerate a cheating man has made me trust men more. Maybe it is because I expect them to cheat at some point. I learned it's not a personal thing, just a man thing.

I may understand men more, but I do not trust women at all. Not one bit. I believe if you are not taking care of your man's needs at home, there is a woman out there waiting with open legs who gladly will. And if it is a woman like me, you can be in trouble because most of the time, it won't be a one night stand. I am smart, sexy, innovative, energetic, optimistic, and give great head. Most cheating men hang around way after the sex has stopped.

With all this lived and learned, I recently started dating again. No more guys with girlfriends, but only single, available men. At twenty-five, I feel it's time I start getting a bit serious about things, especially at a time when my friends are finding boyfriends and evolving as women. I still go out to clubs, but those that attract a more mature crowd. I've also been attending conferences, film festivals, and trying to broaden my social sphere outside the club and my job. I'm through playing with fire and books have become the easiest way for me to escape from the stress of my job.

Reading and spending time (lots of it!) alone has helped me become more in tune with my spiritual self. I am beginning to trust my feelings and becoming comfortable with who I am. I have been working less at NBC and devoting more time to print for a slower pace. I am no longer feeling sorry for myself for having worked so hard to achieve what I have, even if I still don't have a man. It's been almost a year since I had sex. I am doing everything right: abstaining from sex till I get in a serious relationship, meditating, giving to others, and slowing down on the clubs. But I still haven't met a soul I am interested in. Or maybe that person hasn't met me yet? Until then, I'll be practicing patience and picking up another Iyanla Vanzant book.

ALAYA, 27

CITY: San Fran, CA

DATING STATUS: Single, but still looking

Here I am, a year later, still thinking about Keith. The last time I heard, Keith and his girlfriend took a vacation to Saint Barts. I was so devastated. I called Keith and practically begged him to break up with her. He would say things like, "I'm coming back for you," or explain that he really wanted to be with me but couldn't. It's not until now that I have started to wiggle my way out of Keithdom.

However, not speaking to Keith in a while really helped me reflect back on our breakup. I sort of cringe now when I think back to how I acted—so desperate. I was making his day! A beautiful woman calling him all the time, letting him know how special he was, and wanting to be with him. I was probably amusing to him and really inflated his ego! I sometimes wonder if this girlfriend of his was in the background while he was dating me. If he really liked me, wouldn't he have understood me not wanting sex so soon? Why would he just dump me at the first sign of resistance? All of these questions and more make me wonder whether Keith was serious or just another guy trying to dip his hand in the pudding. You figure it out.

I've dated since Keith, but nothing serious. After him, I made a promise that I would never second-guess myself with another man. In keeping with this new approach, I spent the last year having sex with all the wrong guys because I didn't want anyone to slip through my fingers again. This left me with a bag of disappointments and dents in my heart many times. It took the hard way for me to learn that sex is not a prize to be won or an article to be exchanged, but a natural progression in a *healthy,* committed relationship. I always used sex as an exchange article—I gave men sex and they gave me their heart. Sounds dumb? I may have been reading too many romance novels because that way of thinking just set me up to get hurt. And with the little value placed on sex these days, having it with someone you're seeing does not mean commitment. I guess that's all I really wanted—the security of a real relationship.

In the interim, I've been dating only when work permits. It's also so exhausting just trying to get to know someone that I don't want to be bothered half the time. Fernando is determined to see me married by thirty. He has even set me up on blind dates with some attractive men, but most of the time, I don't follow-up. However, there is this one who has been patiently waiting in the "friends zone." We haven't kissed or been alone together after two months of knowing each other. But our attraction is slowly building. We go out once in a while and spend lots of time on the phone on weekend nights. Sometimes, during the silent moments, we can feel our *hearts* growing closer. And that feels good for a change. Fernando thinks Eric may be "the one." And he may be right.

KENYA, 30!
CITY: Miami, FL
DATING STATUS: Engaged

Okay, they say age is nothing but a number. But I was in pain for a while! I felt like my twenties were the best years of my life, and I had nothing to show for it when I turned thirty. It was the most depressing thing, especially after understanding why Gustavo and I broke up. I suffered from the "too good to be true syndrome" that many black women suffer. We think if everything is fine in a relationship, then that means the countdown is on for when the bomb will drop. And since one didn't drop, I created a bomb that destroyed a perfectly good relationship. I was also impatient. I figured time was running out, and I wanted to having my hand in every pot in case I was missing something.

I have not seen anyone since Gustavo—at all! I totally shut down my mind, legs, and heart to men. I left my job after being there nearly eight years. Before quitting I had saved up money and basically just chilled. My condo and car had been paid for two years ago, so there were no rent or car payments to worry about. I basically took the time to just do what I should have done when I was in my mid-twenties! I got my priorities together. I thought life was over after Gustavo, but it was actually the death of one part of my life and the beginning of another.

About four months ago Gustavo called me. His mother would give him messages I would leave like "Hello" and "I miss you." His mother was always respectful, and we always seemed to get along well. My grandmother once told me to always get in good with a man's mother because she will never let him forget you. I wasn't on any fatal attraction moves, but I am a firm believer in out of sight, out of mind. So I wanted to at least stay on his mind if I wasn't in his life. I knew he still loved me but was hurt. When he called me that Friday night, I was breathless. I wanted to play it cool but couldn't. I barely could remember my own name I was so numb with joy. I guess he picked a Friday night to also see if I was at home and not out with someone new.

Gustavo told me that he was basically going through the same thing I was. And he hadn't changed his patrol routes, but they'd put him on desk duty since the sergeant felt he was too edgy or emotional to continue street patrol. However, he's been promoted to detective and loves his new position.

AFTER A LONG TALK, we decided to meet that Saturday. We took a long walk in the park on a breezy, Saturday afternoon. That walk changed my life. After about twenty minutes of cuddling and relaxing on a bench near a playground, Gustavo knelt down by crying babies, old men reading, and kids playing and proposed to me. I practically jumped through that ring—a four-carat diamond ring set in platinum!

His proposing to me that day was something he said he had to do, or he was going to go crazy. Though I'd hurt him, through our time together we had both learned there was no one else in the world for us. Gustavo said he knew he loved me when he tried to continue hating me for sleeping with another man. But after a few months, he was, like me, wondering how I was doing and who I was loving.

However, all the lovemaking we have done has made me two months' pregnant. I became pregnant after he proposed—which I believe is God's way of blessing our reunion. Gustavo and his family are too excited. We have visited my parents in Maryland a few times since we got back together to tell them the news. They were a bit indifferent with Gustavo being Cuban, but they came around eventually when he brought my mother her favorite orchids and my dad authentic Cuban cigars. I still don't talk to them as much, but things are better between us since I am older and settled down.

When I found out I was pregnant, I was surprised and a bit

worried that Gustavo and I wouldn't have enough time alone together after the baby arrived. Our wedding is four months from
now in June and the baby is due in September. Gustavo is in love
with the idea, and his happiness makes me feel a whole lot better.
He comes from a family of seven children, so he feels like he's
getting a head start on things. Plus, at my age, I shouldn't be
waiting much longer for my first child anyway, despite all the
fancy, modern-day conveniences.

I am just in awe about how my life is falling into place. A new
husband, a new baby, a new outlook. I do not plan to go back to
work for a while. I'd like to have about two or three more children
and be a stay-at-home mom and a full-time wife. Gustavo's job
pays very well, and my savings and investments are quite impres-
sive. I eventually would like to work for myself and become a
financial consultant, however, being a wife and mother is first. I
think there is no other role more important or honorable than that
of a mother. It outweighs being the president or CEO of any corporation. And as for the crystals, I don't need them anymore because my request has been answered.

ALEXIS, 26
CITY: Atlanta, GA
DATING STATUS: Dating and "happily single"

Have you ever met a girl who says she doesn't want to be in a
relationship at all? Well, you have now. A year has passed and I

am happily single! Since my little freaky liasons, I feel totally free—mentally, physically, and emotionally. But I've calmed down.

It took me awhile to realize that it was okay to be single. Though I was having mostly sexual relationships with guys like Mike, it was always to fill a void. Having sex gave me that intimacy I was missing from a "real relationship." On the flip side, I got to play out some of my wildest fantasies. I was lucky because I was with guys who respected me. True, I was just a ho to another girl, but to the guy I was just "cool." For instance, Lenox and I would have wild, nasty sex in the back of his car and an hour later, we're chilling in an outside café going over a promotions campaign for his clothing label. Then later, we'll be sucking and licking on each other again. That's the way it worked with almost everyone. I'd always get that phone call, "I need you to help me with something." I guess that's what you get when you have beauty and brains.

I haven't had a boyfriend since Antonio, but I'd rather be happily single than miserably attached. For instance, Renee broke off her engagement three months ago when her fiancé made her get an abortion she was not ready for. His excuse was that he was "just not ready for a baby." The girl is totally devastated! She has no man, and the baby they created is gone. But in all honesty, Renee basically threw herself on that man. When she met him, she moved right in, cooked for him all the time, cleaned for him, and bought him all kinds of jewelry and clothes. The man didn't have enough time to blink before he found himself proposing to her. Actually, she gave him an ultimatum at six months that it was either they plan to get married or move on. The brother was not about to let Renee go after she'd gotten him all dependent on her.

Then she got pregnant. She thought by doing so she could speed things up, but it just blew up in her face. I think he just wasn't ready to be a father, and a husband.

Now Renee is back to hanging with me. I recently moved to New York City to take a job as associate director of Media Relations at a major museum. Renee is finally teaching high-school students at a private school in the city. Living a sheltered life in Atlanta and using sex as a pastime for excitement can all become a little predictable. What better place to sow your wild oats, meet new people, or just basically get into your own than New York? My parents were furious, but at twenty-six they know there is very little they can say. With help from my father, I rented a modest, two-bedroom apartment on the Lower West Side. Renee and I also put our dimes together and got a nice time-share in the Hamptons as well. It's also funny how you see the same group of black people wherever you go in NYC. You can meet a brother at a Saturday night party in Battery Park and see him the next week at NV Tsunami in the Hamptons.

Renee is just finally starting to come out of her shell since her breakup. And all that means is she is starting to get out the house on the weekends. Sometimes I look at Renee since we are the same age and wonder how we can be on such different paths. I'm hoping I can spread the "Pleasures of Being Single" to her:

- Being able to flirt for no reason with the cute guy across the street and when he approaches you, tell him you're taken.
- Being able to wear a cute cowboy hat to tame the wild beast within, a cheetah print bandeau, and a funky metallic skirt

without your man saying, "What the hell you think you doing?"

· Being able to fly to Miami at a last-minute price deal just to
  "swim and get a tan."
· Being able to carefully pick men by their quality instead of
  their looks as one picks fine wine.
· Being able to buy the same pair of Christian Loubouton shoes
  in three different colors without your man giving you a guilt
  trip.

Secretly, I ask myself, "How long will it take to meet the right
person after I tire of being single?" I know doctors, lawyers, and
engineers. The problem is, I've fucked them already. I did get a
phone call recently from Charlton, my "friend" from Atlanta. He
left a whispery message that said he was in town and wanted "to
talk about things." Charlton is president of Myers & Sons, a very
successful construction company in Atlanta that his father started
thirty years ago. It has built some of Atlanta's most prestigious
institutions. Charlton's influence was what got me off the waiting
list of the building I'm in now. I was "seeing" him about three
months ago, but it ended when I decided to come to New York.
We had one of those "having sex and really like each other, but
we don't know what to call it" relationships. If I get back with
Charlton, maybe I can hook Renee up with his twenty-seven-year-
old younger brother. Even if it's just for a friend thing. But for the
meantime, Charlton will be there, and I will be here in New York
single—for now.

WACEERA, 24

CITY: Chicago, IL

DATING STATUS: In an unstable "relationship" still lingering around like an old pain

Laurence and I are not married *yet*. We are still trying to make this relationship work, but it seems like the damage has already been done to both of our abilities to trust the other. Logic and simplicity have been replaced by paranoia, suspicion, and doubt. I would want nothing less than to be able to leave Laurence, but it's like an addiction. I don't want to be alone. And Laurence feels the same way because he hasn't made any moves to dissolve the relationship.

Though things are not perfect, we both have stopped trying to act like everything is fine in the midst of turmoil. Last year, I was just holding my breath until I finally exploded and let him know how I really felt. And at this point, cheating on him is not appealing anymore. If I don't have sex with Laurence, I just don't have sex. I never did tell him about my affairs abroad, but I did confess I'd slept with Lamont. Cooking, cleaning, and taking care of his sexual needs at his requests wasn't enough for him to stay committed; I stopped doing that as often, too.

About four months ago, I caught him with another woman in the car. I ran up to his car while he was laid back getting a blow job and busted the window. The glass scattered everywhere and bruised myself, him, and left his plaything with a bloody arm.

Everyone was quite surprised, even myself. But I wasn't going to let him get away with cheating on me anymore. Laurence convinced the girl not to press charges, and she didn't because her boyfriend would eventually find out. He was blown away by that side of me, and it frightened him. It showed him there was at least one time he was not in control of the situation.

Laurence and I broke up because the stress of that whole car incident was just too much, especially after another faulty promise of trying to be faithful. Shortly thereafter, a fire burned down one of his buildings and left about three hundred thousand dollars' worth of damages. Insurance took care of most of it but left Laurence a bit disillusioned. He called me the same night he heard the news, and we stayed on the phone for hours planning what to do.

It wouldn't be wrong to assume that Laurence needs me more than I need him. I'm his main girl—the trophy type, smart, sexy, attractive, someone he can take out to meet his business associates and at the same time relax at home with in his boxers and T-shirt. Laurence and I have always been on the same level of creativity, achievement, income, and intelligence. He admitted that if I had left him for good, he would feel like he'd lost something irreplaceable. Losing me would have been more like losing a business partner than "just another girl."

On the flip side, the other girls he saw on the side were all demotions—young minded, shallow, materialistic, average or low achievers, but always beautiful. They were happy with a dinner and movie here and there. Laurence always had the satisfaction of having the leverage, that one leg up on the situation. Whereas if he decided to end it, it would be more their loss than his. But according to Laurence and a few weeks of counseling for both of us, that's all in the past.

We *officially* got back together two weeks ago and have not had sex since. Going without sex has been the biggest challenge so far, but we've managed. Our goal is to connect on another level outside of materialism but on something bigger—whatever that may be. I'm twenty-four now, and he'll be twenty-nine in a few days. Time will reveal where our relationship is going, but now we are just trying to float on water.